Assassination Point Blank

A novel by John Onesti

Copyright © 2014 by John W. Onesti

JohnOnesti.blogspot.com

ASSASSINATION POINT BLANK

All rights reserved © 2014 by John Onesti

For information address:

Jonesti13@hotmail.com

ISBN 978-0692334393

Printed in the United States

Assassination Point Blank

Prologue

After his graduation from Harvard, James C. Kelly became a war hero in the Pacific Theatre of World War II, where he saved a member of his squadron in shark infested waters. In the same region, unbeknownst to Kelly, a massive war treasure was discovered by rogue agents of the OSS. Kept secret, the treasure ultimately helped accelerate the growth of a powerful secret espionage establishment which would later threaten his life and the future of America.

At the end of World War II, Kelly hoped the United States' destiny would be to serve as a guiding beacon of freedom and truth to the world. Unlike the colonial empires of Europe, the Communist scourges of the Soviet Union, or the autocratic fascist regimes of the World War II era, Kelly visualized the United States leading the planet by example with integrity, prosperity, innovation, and kindness, instead of a "might makes right" philosophy.

Boyhood illnesses and a serious back injury made worse during the war allowed him to have compassion and view the world through empathic eyes, even though he understood the cold reality that life is not fair. His natural optimism convinced him that every man can rise up to become self-sufficient, productive child of God if given the right environment. After his military service, as he recuperated from back surgery, Kelly decided he would enter the world of politics. He experienced a lucid dream in his hospital bed and set the lofty goal of becoming the President of the United States. After the war, Kelly euphorically believed he could change the world.

Each individual should have inalienable rights and be judged on their own merit not their skin color, where they attended school, their religion, their bloodline, or their membership in some secret organization, Kelly believed. He intended to improve conditions for all Americans and desired to create a legacy as a leader who would leave the world a better place than he found it.

After serving six years in the U.S. House of Representatives, Kelly became elected Senator of Massachusetts in 1953. It was at this time he experienced the power of the media. Being a bachelor may be acceptable for a senator, but not for a man with presidential ambitions. In his thirties and single, Kelly felt compelled to marry. Despite the numerous beautiful women he was seen dating, a news story appeared with a title implying he was gay. The pressure to marry intensified and despite his preference for blondes, he became engaged to Jamie Bene, the brunette newspaper photographer. Their expedient union in 1953 produced two wonderful children and a rocky marriage. Despite the couple's private quarrels, in 1960, on a platform of peace and prosperity, Kelly realized his dream and is elected President.

Chapter 1

The Mysterious Cloud
November 17, 1963

"Mr. Brown, you're here because of your fine record," said the gray haired man interviewing Benjamin Brown. "You're the number one Secret Service agent in our Chicago office. In fact, you're one of the top agents in the nation at bringing counterfeiters and other criminals to trial. I want to commend you." The man's compliments were all facts, but there was something false in all this that Benjamin Brown sensed but did not yet understand.

"Thank you sir," Brown replied, anxious to hear more about the position. He knew the IRS and Secret Service both were under the U.S. Department of the Treasury.

"What we're conducting in the Intelligence Division of the IRS is a top secret, undercover investigation into corrupt activity in Washington, specifically in the Capitol Building."

"What would the position entail for me?" Brown inquired.

"We will place you undercover in the Capitol Building so you can gather intelligence," he said softly as he rolled up the long sleeves of his white shirt. He went on to explain what was required. "There would be an increase in pay, ten percent, but you must change your identity," the gray haired man explained without making eye contact.

"Why?" Brown asked, concerned. It no longer sounded like an interview but rather something more definitive.

"It is necessary. I can't say more than that," the man's eyes shifted down to the papers on his desk.

"When I'm finished would I return to Chicago, back to my job with the Secret Service, and regain my identity?"

"No, this would be a permanent change," for a split second their eyes locked.

"I don't know…" Brown hedged, his face registering concern. The man before him was being evasive. "I need to give this more thought; it's a big decision. Do you mind if I go back to Chicago and discuss it with my wife?"

"That's fine," the interviewer said, but he looked irritated. He wanted an answer, but it was obvious Brown was resolute about waiting and would not give him one on the spot. "We'll talk when you get back to Chicago."

Brown departed the Treasury Building. He smoothly descended the long staircase in the direction of Pennsylvania Avenue, squinting in the bright sunlight of a cloudless day. Rivers of silver light ran through the streets. The gray haired man seemed to be in a hurry to hire him, he mused. Brown was uncomfortable - especially with the idea of changing his identity. Losing his identity was frightening. It felt like something akin to death. He breathed a sigh of relief that at least he told the man he had to think about the offer. It disturbed him that the interviewer was not being completely forthright. Periodically, Brown gazed over his shoulder as he walked. Although he hadn't detected anybody tailing him, he had an eerie feeling of being watched. Filled with a sense of foreboding, he could almost reach out and touch the danger in the air.

He traveled west on Pennsylvania Avenue, then stopped for moment to look south toward the White House. What he saw next utterly disturbed him. His chest tightened. In the distance, framed by a bright blue sky, was the White House. He could see the front gate and the first floor of the building clearly, but the second floor was completely obscured by the presence of a strange thick grey cloud. It ominously covered the upper portion of the White House building, centered directly in front of the President's bedroom window. Brown scanned the horizon - there wasn't another cloud in the sky. It was a bizarre sight indeed. At first he thought he was seeing an illusion or mirage, so he closed his eyes and looked away. He even tried to close one eye at a time, but there again was the cloud, stubbornly covering the upper floors of the building! A chill traveled up Brown's spine. Was it an omen? A harbinger? Whatever the meaning, he could not shake an overwhelming feeling of abject fear.

Brown did not frighten easily. As a boy, his family was poor and he grew up in one of the most dangerous neighborhoods in America. Although well-built and athletic, he was smart enough to know it was better to sidestep trouble when possible. After college he went to work as an Illinois state trooper. His impressive resume had attracted attention after he graduated college summa cum laude.

Despite his physical prowess, Brown learned from experience that there is more to the material world than what one can see with one's eyes or hold in one's hands. When he was a child, he encountered phenomena that could only be explained as supernatural. He had dreams and premonitions as a boy which later came true, some favorable, some not. He was certain that what he was seeing was a portent of impending doom. His own observations on the White House detail told him the president's life could be in danger. The ominous cloud seemed to confirm his fear.

Brown recalled the month he spent protecting President James C. Kelly and his family on the White House detail. It troubled him to remember what he had observed during his stay in Washington. He did his best to warn his superiors in the Agency, but that had come to nothing. Now he had a decision to make. If he took the job and changed his identity, what would become of the old Benjamin Brown, who warned his superiors about the danger to the president? He would be no more! Was that the reason for their eagerness to hire him so quickly? Was he just being paranoid? But what about the mysterious cloud? As he struggled to organize all the simultaneous thoughts rushing through his brain, Brown's memory raced back to June of 1961.

Chapter 2

Inside the Secret Service, June 1961

Like viewing a reel of color film, Brown saw himself as he was two years prior. He remembered vividly his early experiences with the Secret Service; the events appeared as if they transpired the day before.

In the spring of 1961, he met President James C. Kelly for the first time at McCormick Place in Chicago. The President was attending a thank-you dinner given to him by the mayor. In a quiet section of the facility, Brown was assigned to guard a corridor and restroom. Around 8:30, just before the event was to commence, he heard a commotion at the top of a nearby stairwell. Before long, a line of people descended the stairs. Immediately he recognized a man with the handsome looks of a movie star and the unmistakable dignity and stature of a born leader. Walking gracefully toward Brown was none other than President James C. Kelly, followed by Chicago's Mayor Donnelly, the Governor of Illinois, a congressman, and a one of the state's senators. Behind them in the entourage was a long line of local politicians. Arriving at the door of the restroom that Brown was guarding, the President abruptly stopped right in front of him, and with a twinkle in his eye, inquired, "Are you a Secret Service agent or one of Mayor Donnelly's finest?"

Taken by surprise, Brown stared at the President. He could now see Mayor Donnelly standing directly behind President Kelly, wearing an auspicious smile on his face. Brown's large eyes widened. He replied enthusiastically, "I'm a Secret Service Agent, Mr. President. My name is Benjamin Brown."

President Kelly nodded in acknowledgement, having sized up Brown as a good, kind man the moment he spotted him. '*I can sense this man is attentive, reliable, and has a military-like presence; I like him,*' the President thought to himself. '*I could use a man like this in Washington.*'

Then with a Boston accent he asked, "Has there ever been a Negro agent on the Secret Service White House detail, Mr. Brown?"

"I don't think so, Mr. President," Brown shrugged. It was an odd question, but he felt a positive energy.

"Mr. Brown, would you like to be the first?" President Kelly's friendly eyes looked deeply into Benjamin.

"Yes sir, I sure would, Mr. President!" he answered, grinning with excitement. Before meeting him, Brown held President Kelly in high regard. He admired the man's leadership qualities, speaking abilities, and celebrity-like status, but Benjamin now knew beyond a doubt that President Kelly's commitment to racial equality was sincere.

After this short conversation in McCormick Place, Brown was officially invited to serve on the Kelly White House detail. His time there

Assassination Point Blank

confirmed that the President was authentic, the real deal; he was no TV actor. The serendipitous meeting led to Benjamin being assigned for 30 days in Washington DC. He felt he might have the job of a lifetime. When their eyes locked at McCormick Place Brown somehow felt his destiny tied with President Kelly's, but it was impossible to know in what way. Only later, while serving on the White House detail, did he begin to understand how events during his brief service would change his future forever.

* * *

Brown was a realist. Given that he was the first African American to serve with the White House detail, he naturally expected to find some racism. But he was unprepared for the venom within the Secret Service itself. The majority of the White House Secret Service agents were Southerners. A number of them were heavy drinkers and made little effort to hide that fact. During his thirty-day tour, while traveling from the airport to the Kelly family estate in Massachusetts, Agents Rob Forrest, Harry Henders, and several others were still noticeably inebriated from drinking on the flight. The smell of alcohol consumed the car. *These are the men in charge of protecting President Kelly?* Benjamin thought. In his short stay, he witnessed Secret Service agents drinking, partying, and womanizing until all hours of the night.

Brown recalled the evening while he and a team of agents were stationed at a nearby cottage adjacent to the President's father's house, when there was a horrible argument spearheaded by a drunken Harry Henders. Brown remembered it like it was the day before. He and fellow agents Steven Streeter and Sam Smith were sitting on chairs next to a coffee table in the large room of the cottage. They were reading a newspaper under dim lighting, discussing baseball as they checked the box scores of their teams and favorite players in the previous day's games.

"What do you think of the Cubs? Aren't they your team?" Streeter wondered, knowing Brown was from Chicago.

"Yes they are." he answered. "This year I'm especially interested in two young players that I think will turn out to be fantastic, Ron Santo and Billy Williams."

"You know the Orioles are my team," Streeter began to respond. Both men stopped talking as they noticed the card game on the other side of the room was getting loud. Brown realized for the first time that his eyes were watering from the thick cigarette fumes drifting from the vicinity of the card table. He looked over. The smoke was so dense that at times he couldn't see all the men at the table.

"God damn, this is bullshit!" yelled the loud mouth of Harry Henders as he slammed his closed fist on the table with an ear-piercing bang. He was drunk and obviously losing money. All the agents at the table were becoming increasingly obnoxious as the night wore on, especially Henders.

"You know what else is bullshit?" Henders asked angrily with a loud bellow. "The way Kelly is handling integration!"

"You're right about that!" roared agent Forrest.

"Yeah, things were better when we had the General in office," remarked Georgie Blair. Brown was surprised to hear such talk from the men whose job it was to protect President Kelly. He studied Cliff Hillman, the fourth player at the table. Hillman was medium-sized but muscularly built with jet black hair and an olive oil complexion. His Roman nose and icy gray eyes gave him a distinct appearance. These features were typical of a man from a southern Mediterranean ancestry. But Cliff Hillman was an orphan and did not know his true heritage. He remained mostly silent, obviously not wanting to participate in the discussion. Hillman was winning the poker game, quietly cleaning out the others at the table. He remained focused on the money.

"We're going to have another Civil War, if Kelly keeps it up!" continued Henders, his loud voice now shaking the cottage.

Streeter tried to defuse the situation before it got any worse. In an effort to both lighten the mood and change the subject, he shouted toward the table a remark regarding the dismal Washington baseball team, "Hey guys, how about those Senators?" It was too late. By this point Henders was on a rampage. Scowling he looked over to the lounge area of the room where Smith, Brown, and Streeter sat.

"What the hell are you talking about, Streeter? This is no laughing matter! Commies in Cuba and now integration!" he went on, "Kelly doesn't know what he's doing! This country is finished!"

Brown wished he could be invisible. Not knowing what to say or do, he continued to look at the sports section, hoping Henders would stop. He glanced over the top of his newspaper and could see Sam Smith on the couch, hands on his knees, leaning forward. His shoulders were hunched and he was looking at the floor and slowly shaking his head. By this time Henders had gotten up, stumbling his way into the open area of the room where the trio sat.

As Henders made a beeline toward Ben's chair it was obvious where his anger was going to be focused. Next, Henders tried to provoke Brown into a fight. Built like a bull, Henders was broad and stout - not tall, but still wide and intimidating. His face was red with rage and alcohol. Like a madman he waved his arms wildly in the air, his eyes glaring with anger and hatred.

"What are you looking at, Brown? You know you don't belong here, don't you?" he stared with hateful sarcasm. Then, like a rabid animal, Henders took a few steps toward Brown, who by this time was standing up, fists clenched and holding his ground. Realizing Brown was no pushover, Henders became confused and unsure of whether or not to attack. He stopped abruptly and chose to shout racial slurs instead.

Brown's adrenaline flowed through his body and he felt like fighting, but he realized it was not a wise course of action. He was relieved Henders had not come any closer or a violent confrontation would certainly have ensued. Sickened and astonished at Henders' behavior, he walked away onto the porch. A moment later, agent Smith awkwardly came out onto the deck.

Shaking his head in regret and embarrassment, Smith said "Ben, I'm sorry about Harry's behavior. It was totally uncalled for - alcohol tends to bring out the worst in some people. Unfortunately Harry *is* one of those people. He just can't handle his liquor."

It was true. The booze certainly brought Henders' bigotry to the surface. Nevertheless it did not make Brown feel any better about the matter. The unprofessional conduct and prejudice of some of the agents made it obvious to Brown that, despite his enormous admiration for the President, there was no way he could tolerate working on the White House Detail permanently. It would be impossible for him to feel comfortable in such an environment, even if some of the agents like Smith and Streeter were sympathetic to his situation. Perhaps in another ten years it would be a different story, Brown sighed.

As if the Harry Henders episode wasn't bad enough, Brown's observations of the White House detail grew increasingly sinister. The prejudice against him was soon the least of his worries. One evening, he again overheard some of the agents openly expressing their complaints about President Kelly. They reiterated that Kelly was somehow ruining the country and they even went as far as to say that if shots were fired on the President that they would take no action to protect him. He could still remember the incident. It stuck with Brown and haunted him.

The voices remained in his head, "That god-damned Kelly," one agent complained. "He's screwing up this country. That Catholic Mick is putting his nose in places it doesn't belong!"

"That's right," chimed in another. "And the worst part is we have to protect the s.o.b."

"Well, if he's shot at, I'm not sure I would be in a hurry to do anything. It's gotten so bad I've even thought about quitting," one veteran agent bemoaned. Brown was surprised and distressed to hear such remarks expressed openly. The safety of President Kelly became an ongoing source of consternation for Brown.

He reflected on the stupendous paradox regarding the attitudes of these Secret Service agents. President Kelly, he discovered, actually treated the men better than any President before him. Kelly was much more personable and friendly in his interactions with his agents than any President in recent memory. Unlike the previous President, who simply called out to all the men around him 'hey agent,' Kelly actually went out of his way to get to know the men. But that didn't matter; certain men in the agency had made up their minds that they hated him. When necessary they could behave like the professionals they once were, but at the end of the day they were a dangerous enemy within.

On top of the serious character problems of some of the agents, Brown also found the training to be unsatisfactory. Whenever he had a question, the other agents almost always answered by saying, "we all learn on the job." Once he was handed a semi-automatic rifle and when he told a fellow agent he hadn't been trained on how to operate the gun, the agent just smiled and said, "Just pretend that you know."

The after-dark carousing and drinking of the agents was so egregious that Brown wondered whether the men on duty the following day would be in condition to protect President Kelly even if they wanted. The atmosphere was more like a college fraternity house than an elite group of finely-trained agents: much different than Brown had envisioned.

***

Later that week, Brown tried his best to focus his thoughts on the positives of his experience on the detail. He recalled how he met Scott Kelly, the President's younger brother and the Attorney General. One day he was on duty patrolling the beach as President Kelly was out on his yacht. The boat returned to the dock and as President Kelly began walking along the beach he spotted Brown and called him over.

"Mr. Brown, come on over, I'd like you to meet my brother Scott," he said with a smile.

Scott Kelly nodded with approval and extended his hand.

"Pleased to meet you, Mr. Brown, my brother told me that you two met in Chicago and that you are the first Negro on the White House detail. I'm happy to see that progress is being made."

After their introduction, Scott Kelly inquired about Brown's past, his family and his career goals. He even made some suggestions for Ben to consider for improving his advancement opportunities. And like his older brother, his interest was genuine. Benjamin immediately took a liking to both men. His instincts told him that the Kelly brothers were good, honest, patriotic men, the kind of men that he was proud to serve and protect. He also noticed their differences, which went beyond the obvious physical attributes. Scott was younger, more slightly built, and a few inches shorter. They had the same chestnut brown hair, and one could easily tell that they were brothers. James Kelly's eyes were larger, rounder, and more sympathetic and friendly in appearance than his younger brother's. Personality-wise it was obvious that Scott Kelly was far more high strung, intense, and competitive than the President. He did not have the same sense of humor, diplomacy, or compassion as his older brother. But their differences actually provided a synergy which made them even better. Together they were a strong team. Brown could hear some of the conversation as the two brothers strolled up the sloping beach toward the house.

"Scott, I can never know exactly what it is like to be Mr. Brown, but I can imagine. Take our situation: 25% of our country is Catholic and yet the media made a big deal out of our religion in 1960. It's especially interesting because when I fought in the South Pacific, nobody cared about my religion."

"It's going to take time, James but I'm happy to see Mr. Brown here. It reassures me that changes are occurring, even if it is at a slow pace."

"Scott, I try to view things through other peoples' perspectives and take each person as an individual. Protecting the individual's rights is essential and I have no problem using the Federal powers for this purpose."

"It's the only way."

"And I know that with all the turmoil we have in the world right now, it's not going to be easy. It hasn't been. But that is why I selected you as my Attorney General. Because I knew you were the only one tough enough for the job. And I knew you would never quit," he said as he glanced proudly at his younger brother at his side.

Walking directly into the sun, deep in thought, Scott said, "I'm convinced if we get two terms in office, we're going to solve the problems of this country."

***

"I heard you were leaving today" Steven Streeter said with a sad look on his face as he stopped Brown just before his flight back to Chicago. After thirty days on the White House detail, Brown had decided to return to the Chicago office. "I have something for you." He handed Brown a small object. It was a tie clip. But it was no ordinary tie clip. It said "Kelly 1960" on it. "It's for good luck, Ben. I'm sorry it didn't work out for you here. I wish you would stay, we could use another good man here, but I understand why you're going back."

"I can't take this Steve," Brown replied.

"You don't understand. I want you to have it." It was obvious Streeter had gone well out of his way to find Brown so that he could have the tie clip.

"Thanks Steve, I'll always remember this gesture."

"All God's best back in Chicago, Ben." Streeter smiled at Brown, turned and headed back to his post.

***

During his exit interview from the White House detail, which ironically was in the same Treasury Building where he would later meet the grey-haired man, Benjamin reported all of his findings to the chief of the Secret Service. The chief was, unbeknownst to Brown, on his way out. He was retiring after over 30 years of service. In fact, as he was conducting Brown's exit interview, he was shuffling through his office belongings in an effort to determine which items he could take home early because he would be vacating the post in less than a month. He half-listened to Brown's concerns, but action didn't seem likely.

Later that afternoon a despondent Brown boarded a plane back to Chicago. Peering dejectedly out a nearby window he fidgeted around uncomfortably in his seat the entire trip. When he finally arrived in Chicago he felt as if he had just finished a rugged football game. His muscles were tight and aching, and that night he could not sleep much despite being exhausted. He told his wife before going to bed, "It is one thing for me to find prejudice on the job; but to discover the president's life is in danger – talk about depressing!"

* * *

Brown's concerns for President Kelly hung heavily around him. He informed his superiors in the Chicago office about the seriousness of the situation in Washington. His bosses in Chicago were sticklers when it came to the rules. They were shocked to hear about the agents' drinking on the job because it was strictly against policy. In Chicago, they tried to operate as much as possible by the rules in the Secret Service manual. However, when Brown began to discuss the discrimination problems in the organization their focus then seemed to shift away from the White House detail agents' excessive drinking and negligence to Benjamin being so "thin skinned" and "sensitive." The topic of discrimination diverted his superiors' attention away from the poor job the men on the

White House detail were doing in providing security for President Kelly.

Brown's objective was to disclose all of his findings concerning the White House detail. He believed his testimony revealing the bigoted men in Washington would bolster his argument. It would provide supporting evidence proving the men were of questionable character and judgment, he thought. Brown was wrong: it had the opposite effect. His superiors, uncomfortable with the topic of discrimination, distanced themselves from the entire situation. As soon as the subject came up in conversation they no longer saw the big picture and the importance of Brown's observations; their perspective and priorities became clouded. The president's life remained in danger.

Chapter 3

A Giving Man, summer 1963

Steven Streeter stood at attention as he guarded the doorway leading into the office of President Kelly's secretary, Ellen Lakeland. He could not hear the entire conversation but the discussion about tie clips brought back his memory of Ben Brown. Over two years had passed since he had given Brown his going away present. He peeked at his watch. President Kelly's day was winding to a close.

"Mr. President, the '64 election is fast approaching. The campaign sent over a box of tie clips like the ones we had during 1960," Ellen told President Kelly. "Last time they were a big hit."

Streeter glanced over his shoulder to observe Ellen Lakeland for a moment. Conservatively dressed in an outfit that buttoned to her neck, she sat with a straight, rigid posture. As usual, her dark hair was a mess but that didn't matter, in her middle fifties, she was not employed for her pretty face. With Ellen Lakeland, President Kelly had a personable secretary and a master of organization and efficiency. The phone rang and out of the corner of his eye Streeter could see her warm smile as she answered. While on the phone, she adjusted her horn-rimmed glasses and reached for a folder. Lakeland was a woman who cared more about the papers on her desk than the tidiness of her hair. Meticulous about the important details of her job, she could handle any project the President sent her way. Her massive mahogany desk was situated between President Kelly's office and the Cabinet Room.

***

Ellen Lakeland's experience went way back. When she was a girl, her father served in Congress. The experience made her comfortable and familiar with Washington protocol. Her employment with James Kelly began while he was still a congressman. At that time he was a long shot campaigning for the Senate against an established opponent. Even then she realized that he was different from the other men on Capitol Hill. She recognized him as a rising political star. Her intuition proved correct and today she was working in the White House as Personal Secretary to the President. Now that he was the President of the United States he continued to make Ellen proud to work for him.

"Mr. President, there is someone here to see you." Ellen said as she entered his office, noticing he was working hard at his desk. "It's Mae Smith's friend, Charlotte Thompson, from England. I can tell her you're unavailable if you wish," Ellen said to the president who began to rise from his desk. "I know you have a full schedule, do you want me to have her wait?"

"No, no, that's ok Ellen. I need to take a break from all this paperwork anyway and clear my mind," he said as he set down his pen and headed toward her office. Seeing the identity of his guest, a friendly smile appeared on his face. It was an elderly woman of about 90.

"Mr. President, this is Charlotte Thompson," Ellen made the introduction.

"Good day Mr. President," the old lady said in a heavy British accent, shuffling her feet toward him to shake his hand.

"Pleased to meet you, Ms. Thompson," replied the president. He could already tell his appearance had made the old woman's day as a wide grin appeared on her wrinkled face. She was a close family friend of his children's nannie, Mae Smith. Smith had mentioned the old woman and how she was a huge fan of his.

"I wanted to meet you and Mae said she'd do her best," the old lady said slowly in a weak, high pitched voice.

"Mae always comes through," the president joked, "you know she has to watch my daughter and junior; that's a handful in itself."

"I hope I didn't interrupt your work."

"No, not at all, your timing was perfect. You came all that way from England to see me? Wow, we should get a picture," the president laughed.

"I'll find a photographer," Ellen said on her way out of the room. Seconds later she was back with a White House photographer. He proceeded to take several photos of the president and his elderly fan from England. Kelly autographed an existing photo.

"We'll have the ones I just took developed and send them to you," the photographer explained to the old lady. Charlotte Thompson left the office that afternoon with a look of a woman who had just won the sweepstakes. Such kind gestures were what set President Kelly apart from men in similar positions.

Ellen had witnessed countless instances where James Kelly had gone far out of his way to acknowledge, thank, or do something considerate for people who were amazed that the President of the United States, as busy as he was, could maintain such clarity of mind to remember and take time for them. Consequently he was admired and loved. Ellen couldn't possibly count how many letters they received from people saying, "You'll never know how much your thoughtfulness has meant to me." Kelly believed that because he represented the people his door should always be open.

Ellen Lakeland recalled the numerous occasions in which James Kelly had proven to be an impressive thinker and true man of the people. She was present during all the well known instances demonstrating his strong independence as a Senator. She saw how at times he refused to go along with his party, the Democrats, if he felt they were mistaken and how he would vote with the Republicans when he thought they were right. As a result of his family's wealth and his personal integrity, President Kelly was not beholden to outsiders to the extent of other Senators who were rumored to be indebted to those who helped them ascend to power. When he received letters from his constituents he read them all and paid special attention to those that were critical. From those, he told Ellen, he often learned the most.

On the evening of Charlotte Thompson's visit, Ellen Lakeland and President Kelly had finally completed their office work and schedule of appointments for the day. On his desk was a list of charities that had received his Presidential salary the year before. Each year he donated his entire salary of $100,000 to various charities because he genuinely wanted to help the less fortunate. He had also laid the groundwork to form an organization beneficial to the impoverished worldwide. Some in his inner circle had advised him to make public the generous charitable gifting of his Presidential salary, saying it would be an astute political move. However Kelly explained that his giving was not motivated by approval ratings. His giving was a matter between himself and God.

The President buzzed Ellen. She rose from her desk, appearing in the doorway to his office. The room was so spacious that she was in the habit of walking halfway across the carpet toward his desk in order to have a normal conversation.

"Yes Mr. President?" She noticed that he was holding back laughter, a wide grin on his face. "What is so funny?"

"I was just thinking about years ago when you first began working for me. Remember that time when I left my office and there was a huge stack of papers on my desk? And when I returned you had tidied everything up and filed them all away?"

"Yes, I do. And you buzzed me into your office angry about it because I straightened up your desk and filed everything! I was just trying to help organize things." Ellen said clearly recalling the day twelve years earlier. She was aware that the President was kidding with her and reminiscing fondly to the time when he was new to politics. He was rarely in a bad mood but on that day he was in pain from his back injury. He quickly came to realize that Ellen was one of the best secretaries in Washington and that he was lucky to have her.

"I had my own system of finding things back then," he said with a laugh. "And you messed everything up! Well on that day my back was hurting and just about everything bothered me. But the reason I bring it up is because I wanted to thank you again for all the wonderful work you have done for me over the years. You have made my journey in politics much smoother."

Ellen was happy to hear his words of praise. Concerning his back troubles, she could relate and sympathize with him since she had serious back problems of her own. A tumor near her spine had to be removed. Making matters more complex, it was dangerously close to the nerves. After a life saving surgery her doctors thought she might never walk again, but over time and with God's help she proved them wrong. The surgery and rehabilitation forced her to miss significant time at work, but miraculously with the aid of her husband, friends and a strong will she recovered.

During the time of Ellen's absence a feeling of melancholy overhung James Kelly's office. He was saddened by her illness and even after her recovery he wasn't sure if it was wise for her to return to her demanding, stressful position. But she insisted, saying that there was no place she would rather be than to get back to her assignments. She knew that he valued her work and admired her courage and determination. It was a mutual respect and appreciation that grew even stronger after her surgery and long recovery. She was always thankful to have him as her boss. In fact, she repeatedly told her husband that there was no other official in Washington D.C. for whom she would rather work.

Turning to leave his office she kiddingly retorted, "Is that what you buzzed me in here for?" While departing his prodigious office, she stopped in the doorway to ask Kelly, "Mr. President, did you get a chance to look at that list of charities from last year? Are you thinking of making any changes this year?"

"Yes Ellen," President Kelly nodded. His large empathic eyes looked up from his shuffling through the remaining papers on his desk. "There is one charity I would like to add so we need to modify the allocation percentage around, but otherwise I am happy with last year's group," he said as he continued to scan the remaining paperwork.

Also on his desk was the financial report received earlier in the afternoon from Madeline Murphy, the First Lady's secretary, detailing his wife Jamie's expenses. Ellen detected a growing change of expression on the President's face, and instantly she knew that he was viewing Murphy's report. She had been around him for twelve years and there were only three things that could get President Kelly in a sour mood: a world conflict, a painful back, or his wife's expense report. It was a long day, and he now was standing up shaking his head in disgusted amusement as he flipped through the papers of the report. Ellen was aware that the First Lady's spending, especially on her clothing, was wildly out of control.

"Another dress?" she remarked knowingly.

"More than one, and how did you guess?" He answered as he closed his briefcase. "Have a good night, Ellen. I'll see you tomorrow morning," he said, and headed for the door.

"See you tomorrow, Mr. President."

Chapter 4

Old Friends, summer 1963

The President's ninety-two foot yacht cruised along the dark blue waters off the coast of Massachusetts. Peter "Red" Farleigh stood smiling on its deck. His white golf shirt was neatly tucked into his dark pants, which he had anchored high above his waist. President Kelly piloted the vessel while Farleigh stood nearby enjoying the fresh air and open water. Kelly was only two inches taller than Red, but his thick hair gave the impression that he was even taller. Because of his Irish coloring, President Kelly referred to Peter as "Red." Even more than his red hair, Farleigh's personality made him a standout. He hit it off with just about everyone.

"Take a look at this, Red." As he continued to pilot the yacht, the president pulled an envelope of photos out of the drawer of a nearby cabinet. He handed Red a picture. It was the two of them on the golf course in the summer of 1960, while Kelly was still a senator campaigning for the presidency. "We did it in '60 Red, and we'll do it again!" Over the years Red had helped his friend with his political campaigns and now Kelly had been president for almost three years.

"Here's one from 1942," Kelly said as he handed Red another.

"Wow, talk about a walk down memory lane," Red replied. It was a photo of the two men as lieutenants in the Navy. It dawned on Red that they had been friends for over twenty years, more than twice as long as the President had been married. Time had advanced too quickly, thought Farleigh.

Farleigh recalled the early 1940s when they spent their days together in the U.S. Navy. During World War II they served on PT boats in a squadron in the South Pacific. He thought about how lucky he was to have James Kelly as a close friend. It was a fortuitous meeting during a pickup football game. Despite being from opposite coasts they had similar upbringings. Both were raised in Irish-American families. Having grown up in California, Farleigh had been a stranger to Washington politics, but he was no dummy. He had graduated from the prestigious Stanford University and had met his share of intelligent and capable men, but none that could compare with James C. Kelly. Kelly was a superstar, the complete package. A Harvard graduate, he had good looks, intelligence, unusually strong magnetism, integrity, and tremendous leadership skills. When he walked into a room he had the aura of someone special, and everyone felt it. Men liked and respected him, and women adored him.

"By the way, how's your Dad doing?" the President asked.

"The old man's great. Of course he still wishes I was in California helping him with the construction business, but he knows my work with you is important. You know, of all my friends you're the only one who hit it off really well with the old man."

The President found the remark amusing, knowing it was true. He recognized Red's father was a serious, hard-nosed man, the type of man who wants the best for his children but can be overbearing and critical. To Red's amazement, somehow the first time Peter Farleigh Sr. met James Kelly, he liked him. The stern demeanor dropped and he was laughing and having fun immediately. He told his son later that he found James Kelly to be intelligent and engaging. The old man's compliments, though rare, were generally accurate. James Kelly loved people and had one of the most brilliant minds Peter had ever encountered. He could read and comprehend as fast as anyone Peter had met.

"Red, do me a favor. Read that article," Kelly asked as he pointed to an article circled in the newspaper sitting on a nearby shelf. After a few moments of watching Peter read, Kelly became impatient, saying jokingly, "Red, what the heck are you doing? Memorizing it? Come on; I'm the President of United States. I don't have all day!" The President had a pleasant sense of humor and enjoyed joking around, but Peter recognized his old friend valued time more than any commodity, especially now that he was in the oval office and didn't have much to spare.

"It looks like the reporter doesn't like you," Red said, pointing out the obvious.

"It's worse than that, Red. Information is still leaking out. How did the reporter know some of the information in the article?" Kelly asked, suggesting the presence of a mole in his administration.

Peter reread the article. Sure enough he saw what Kelly meant. He knew the Kelly's were at odds with the media.

"I see what you mean," Red replied, contemplating the implications.

"Now, you can see why I've continually had to clean house." Kelly said, referring to the personnel changes.

"I do. It's disturbing," Red replied, not knowing what else to say. Cloak-and-dagger topics were not his specialty.

"I'll give you more details later," Kelly said, realizing it was not the right time. "Anyway, look at this one," Kelly was now holding another photo. "It's one of you at my birthday party, singing that Hollywood song of yours. You sure had everyone cracking up," the President said, examining the photo for a moment.

It was a photo of Red standing with a microphone singing his satirized song about Hollywood to the guests at the party. A natural entertainer and comedian, Farleigh was acting as the master of ceremonies that night. It was easy for him; in school he was always both the smart guy and the class clown rolled into one. Those attributes made him both valuable and likeable.

"Speaking of Hollywood, have you seen any good movies lately? The last time I went out to see a movie was a couple years ago with you."

"You're not missing anything."

"Sometimes Jamie and I will watch a movie in the White House theatre, but she always picks strange ones."

"Like what?"

"She likes foreign heartbreakers, like *Last Year at Marienbad, Jules et Jim, Black Tights,* and *Walk on the Wild Side.*"

"I've never heard of any of those," Red laughed. It came as no surprise that the eccentric Jamie would have unusual taste in movies.

"Tragic love triangles. Someone always ends up dead, usually the husband," Kelly laughed.

Red looked behind and noticed a Secret Service agent in a boat behind them. Now that Kelly was president, he and his companions were continually shadowed by Secret Service agents. Even when he would take his yacht out there would normally be an agent on board and a few more trailing in another vessel. President Kelly didn't mind the men being around and he never interfered with their job duties or requests. In fact, though it was obvious many agents held different political views, President Kelly liked the men and took great interest in their personal lives, more than any President before him. The previous President, a former Army General, kind of a cold fish, had never made attempts to get to know the agents. Instead he ordered them around, never calling

them by name. It wasn't unusual to hear him
bark, "hey agent, come over here."

"How has Jamie been feeling lately?" Red
asked, knowing Kelly's wife was about 6-7
months pregnant.

"So far, so good," Kelly replied.

Both men were silent, then finally Kelly
spoke. "By the way Red, when I was in El Paso I
saw your old boss."

Red was thunderstruck for a second. He
immediately recognized that the President was
talking about Ron Conway, now the Governor of
Texas, who used to hold the position of
Secretary of the Navy. Red had worked beneath
Conway briefly after he had taken the job of
Under Secretary of the Navy. Red later learned
that Conway, and his long time mentor, former
Texas Senator Lionel Jones, now the Vice
President, had been pushing for one of their
men to have the position. It was obvious that
Vice President Jones had pressed President
Kelly to hire Conway as the Secretary of the
Navy. Even worse, Jones and Conway also wanted
to pick the man for the Under Secretary
position as well. Trying to strike a
compromise, Kelly had asked Red if he would
accept a lesser position of Assistant Secretary
of the Navy. But Red had already committed to
his family that he would only accept the Under
Secretary position. Even the discussion of
taking the position of Under Secretary of the
Navy had caused an uncomfortable rift within
his family, especially with the old man, who
felt Red's presence in California was essential

for the family to continue running the construction company his father had founded. No way was Red about to drop a notch and take Assistant Secretary of the Navy position. To leave the family business for anything less than the Under Secretary of the Navy seemed insulting to the old man.

In the end, President Kelly felt that he had made numerous concessions and had given plenty of jobs to Jones's people. He wanted some men he could trust implicitly around him. He stood firm this time, and Red was named Under Secretary of the Navy, the position right below Conway. It was a classic Washington conundrum: even a likeable, honest and patriotic person like Red would create adversaries. His simple willingness and commitment to serve the President put him on the wrong side of Jones and Conway. They didn't figure in Red's steadfastness at the time, but they would never forgive him. Given an inch they would take a mile.

Red couldn't miss the fact that Ron Conway, Vice President Jones, and even Roderick McNeil, the Secretary of Defense, did not want him to have the post. He could sense it even during interviews. Kelly was trying to please everyone, and Red was in the awkward position of proving that impossible. Things got uncomfortable all the way around. As soon as he met them, Jones and Conway struck Red as the kind of men who were never happy. Regardless of how much power they had, their thirst for more could never be quenched.

In 1961, the day before Red's swearing-in, he asked Ron Conway if he could go up to New York to inspect a damaged air craft carrier. His wife and daughter were in New York, and it would be convenient if they could ride back on the Navy plane to Washington for the ceremony. Conway gave Red the all-clear.

The airplane had a mechanical failure while in mid-flight and lost power. It was forced to crash land in an estuary. Although everyone aboard was alright, the incident caused a cascade of complications. The near miss was especially emotional for the president because he had lost his older brother, William Kelly Jr. in a plane crash during World War II. As the president saw the situation, losing a good friend would have been tragic enough – but with that plane a lot of general public support would have crashed.

It was unbecoming for the not yet Under Secretary of the Navy to be flying around with his wife and child aboard, certainly not standard protocol. Kelly was upset with Red and even more so with Conway for approving the use of the plane. Both men should have known better.

The accident became a point of contention for the president and Conway. Conway's stay as Secretary of the Navy was short - less than a year before he left to run for Governor of Texas. And Red knew he dodged a bullet that day on the Navy plane. In his gut Red always had a creepy feeling about the plane crash.

The wind picked up and the boat bounced. To maintain his balance Red reached for a grab rail as the vessel rocked on some choppy waves. "When I was down in El Paso I promised him I would return this fall," continued the President. "A lot of people are lamenting about the division within the Democratic Party in Texas. The governor thinks that my presence might help patch up the feud between the various contingents of the party. And like it or not, Texas is crucial for my reelection."

As he listened to the President, Peter saw an old lighthouse flickering dimly on the shoreline and he could feel the boat turning as the President began to head back to port. Red thought about Texas. It was common knowledge that the Democratic Party there had issues. He wasn't certain what the wily Conway was up to, but there was no doubt the Governor had big money behind him.

The tall Texan was a slick, ambitious man who had faithfully helped his mentor, Lionel Jones, move up the ladder of Texas politics. Jones had become the most powerful man in the U.S. Senate before he accepted the Vice Presidency. For many years, Conway had done a masterful job of running Jones' election campaigns in Texas almost always with success being the result. And even though Kelly often acknowledged it, Jones enjoyed holding over the President's head his strength in the south, which helped Kelly get elected. When Jones agreed to be Kelly's running mate he aggressively horse-traded in bringing his friends into the new administration.

Perhaps Jones and Conway were already contemplating as far ahead as the 1968 elections and Conway's potential position of President or Vice President, Farleigh surmised. In any case, Farleigh cynically sensed an insidious motive.

Texas had a long history of feuds in the party, so why was a presidential visit so imperative now? Red thought. He remembered how when Kelly and Jones were running against each other in the primary, Conway was Jones' campaign manager and had tried to stress that Americans should think twice about electing James Kelly because of his history of Addison's disease: "if elected, he might not live out his term."

By this time the President had maneuvered the boat in the direction of home and was already thinking of all the work waiting for him upon his return. Red was more talkative earlier in the trip but the mention of Conway stalled the conversation.

Misgivings about the corruption and manipulation of the Texans ran through Red Farleigh's thoughts as he spoke, unable to hide his contempt for them. "You know James, I don't understand politics very well, and I hate to say it, but a lot of those Texans are bad news. It seems like there is always an ulterior motive or strings attached every time they do business."

"I understand how you feel Red. They're pretty demanding, but that's just politics in Texas. There are a lot of fine, honest people down there. Hey, I have some work to do tonight, but what do you say we go golfing tomorrow morning?"

"Sounds grand! Let's do it." Red replied with a faint grin, trying to forget about the slick Governor.

The President further tried cheering Red up by telling a joke. "Yesterday I asked my wife what she wanted for Christmas. She said 'a divorce.' I said I wasn't planning on spending that much." Sure enough it worked; even the though in some ways the joke was not far from reality, it raised a smile from Farleigh, who was fully aware of Jamie's luxurious taste and the fact that she threatened to divorce James Kelly repeatedly.

"We'll play early in the morning; after lunch I'm flying back to Washington." Then the irresistible smile, "You know Red; someday you'll have to write a book about your times with the President." Kelly loved to joke with Red about being the President. It was an inside joke. They'd known each other for over 20 years and despite his obvious talents, Red sometimes couldn't believe his friend had made it that far. He remembered back to the time James Kelly had told him, while they were both still in the Navy, that one day he would be the President of the United States. And as incredible as it was,

two decades later, his friend had made good on
that prediction and brought his old pal Red
along for the ride!

Chapter 5

Father, Gentleman and Patriot

President Kelly was on the floor playing with his children, Cathy and James Jr. It was still summer and months before Halloween but the two were in costumes. Cathy was dressed as a witch and carried a black kitten while James Jr. was a scary monster with fur like a gorilla and a pointy hat. They were giggling behind their masks, but the President was laughing even more. James Jr. had wanted to scare his Daddy, but inadvertently scared himself for a moment, causing his plan to backfire. At first it upset him that he failed to frighten his Dad, but being a good-natured boy he quickly resumed his rambunctious play with his father and sister as they romped around Kelly's office.

Whenever possible, President Kelly carved out time for his children. They loved playing with him. Their English nanny, Miss Smith, knew that each time the children heard his helicopter approach for landing they would be overcome with excitement, especially James Jr. They would always want to run out to greet him, or at least go to a nearby window to watch. She did her best to accommodate them so they could spend as much time with him as possible. Remarkably, even with all the pressure he always wore a smile.

Both children were well-behaved and not the least bit spoiled considering their circumstances. Mae Smith saw to that. She had worked as a nannie all over the world and always knew just how to handle children. The difference in their personalities was something she picked up on at once. She noticed how James Jr. was a lot like his father in that he was outgoing and lovable and a bit of a jokester. One couldn't help but like him, even when he was getting into trouble or acting up, as he sometimes did. Cathy was more reserved and soft spoken. She was a bright little girl but didn't have the straightforward and comical demeanor of her brother. She thought things through carefully before she spoke. Their favorite common interest was their father, who Cathy called Silly Daddy because he was always teasing her and acting goofy whenever they could get together and play.

On this day Mae Smith was sitting near the wall on a small hard-backed chair in the President's office. Though she had worked for the Kelly family for over seven years, she was always amazed with the President's memory, ability to focus, and his consideration even while under immense pressure and distractions. And more impressive was his even keeled demeanor no matter the circumstances. In all her time with the family Mae could not recall him ever losing his temper. The President was the rare combination of success, celebrity, and down to earth simplicity.

Assassination Point Blank

"Hello, Miss Smith," he said smiling at her while playing with his children next to a desk full of books and papers. "Is that the most comfortable chair you can find to relax on?"

"Oh, I'm fine, Mr. President," she replied.

Nevertheless, the President stood up to pull over a more comfortable chair for Miss Smith to sit on while she watched him and his children play. She was a couple of decades his senior and she admired his respect for older people.

"Miss Smith, Jamie and I want to thank you for the wonderful job you've done with our children. I really appreciate the excellent care you've been giving them. Even I am surprised at how respectful and well mannered they are, considering they are the children of the President." He smiled with a wide grin. "I'm sure my mother told you that her children, especially the boys, were always driving her crazy and getting into all types of mischief." He said with a laugh.

"Thank you Mr. President, but I do think that some of the credit is just the demeanor of the children. I like to think that with all my experience that I know how to handle youngsters, which is partly the case, but they are intelligent and they both have pleasing personalities which certainly makes my job easier, so I would like to return the compliment to your family as well. And James Jr. is so amusing; he always has something funny up his sleeve. I love my job. It's a joy to be around them."

Assassination Point Blank

It was true. The entire staff loved the children because they were not only cute and funny but they treated all adults with respect. They actually made the staff's job more fun when they were around.

As Miss Smith finished her last sentence, Jamie and Madeline entered the room.

"Miss Smith, could you please take the children out of here, right away. Their voices are piercing my ears," Jamie said in an annoyed tone. "And have them change out of those costumes."

"Yes, Mrs. Kelly, right away. Come along," Miss Smith motioned to the children and they hurried out of room. Cathy was right behind her nanny, but young James was lollygagging a bit because he wanted to continue playing with his father. It wasn't uncommon for Jamie to quickly lose her patience with them and then call on Miss Smith whenever this occurred.

For the most part, Miss Smith got along well with the first lady. Perhaps it was because being from England she was accustomed to dealing with British blue bloods. Unfortunately the same could not be said for most of the other help. Mrs. Kelly's demanding requests and knack for changing decisions on a whim had them all walking on egg shells and drove some of the help to pack up and leave. She could also be cheap, making the help work overtime and refusing to give raises if at all possible. In the six years Mae Smith spent with the Kelly family she couldn't remember how many times she heard Jamie tell her secretary,

Madeline, "Can you please call the employment service and see how soon we could have a replacement?" It was like a revolving door. Cooks seemed to have the greatest turnover, but the same was true with other servant positions as well. So much so that part of Madeline's job responsibilities was specifically to deal with servant problems. She was better at smoothing over hurt feelings than Jamie was at apologizing.

As she took the children up to their rooms to change, Miss Smith thought about personalities and realized that in all likelihood, James Jr. would grow up to be active, outgoing and extroverted like his father. He possessed the same sensitive nature and a similar kind of self-confidence and charm. Cathy though more reserved and measured in her interactions was also kind and sensitive to others feelings. They both were like their father Miss Smith thought thankfully.

Chapter 6

America's Queen

On the second floor of the White House, Madeline Murphy made her way toward the Queen's Suite, named for the royal guests it hosted over the years. The spacious Queen's Bedroom, Queen's Sitting Room and Queen's Bath, were freshly adorned in bright, busy French fabrics. From the stair landing she could hear a baritone voice. The first lady was trying on clothing with her fashion designer, the internationally renowned Vosco Cassone. Madeline cut through the East Hall adjacent to the Queen's Bedroom. As she poked her head in the sitting room she could see Jamie Kelly surrounded by her designer Vosco Cassone, his assistant, the first lady's maid, and a riot of textiles. It looked as if a color bomb had gone off in the middle of the room.

"No, not this one," Jamie said to Vosco as she unzipped an apricot tweed.

"Try this one next," suggested Vosco as he handed her a lush green sequinned dress.

Madeline's entry went unnoticed as the others were consumed in their activities. The suite was in total disarray. The furniture was pushed back against the walls and clothing was scattered throughout the room. Dresses were draped over antique furniture, and dangling from hangers at the windowsills. Ladies shoes were strewn about the floor and a convoy of brass luggage carts sat in the center of the room like gypsy wagons, still overflowing with Vosco Cassone's inventory.

The only area of the room with any organization whatsoever was the blue sofa where Vosco and his assistant Kimberly arranged outfits a few at a time for the first lady's inspection. Jamie's Dominican maid, Maria, futilely tried to bring order to the little carnival, but every time she was sent to fetch another pair of shoes or earrings from Jamie's dressing room, the chaos would return like a tide.

Jamie abandoned the apricot dress on the floor. Enthusiastically she grabbed two others Vosco suggested and left him and his assistant for the Queen's Bath.

"Maria, the satin shoes are not here. Some are in the other bedroom, could you please find them?" The first lady had so much clothing that it was stored in several rooms.

"Yes, right away, Mrs. Kelly," Maria said playing catch-up as she picked a few items off the floor before rushing off to find the shoes. "One good thing about this job is it keeps me slim," Maria thought as she scooted down the hall.

As she left the sitting room, Maria noticed Madeline watching the proceedings from the doorway. They exchanged a look as Maria brushed past. The first lady emerged this time in a black dress Cassone knew she would love.

Assassination Point Blank

"What do you think?" Vosco Cassone asked with one hand on his chin as he studied the first lady.

"*Cette robe est magnifique. Je le veux!"* Jamie smiled. She loved it. She spoke fluent French. After attending Vassar College for two years she spent her junior year in France on an exchange program through Smith College, one of Vassar's sister schools.

Madeline realized there was no hope of interrupting the proceedings, and retreated to handle the first lady's mail at her little antique desk in the Monroe Room. Sadly, Jamie had lost a newborn baby just a couple weeks earlier and Madeline was glad to see the first lady in better spirits. Vosco Cassone's dresses always lifted Jamie's mood.

A half hour later Madeline returned. She noticed Jamie's "purchase cart" groaning under the weight of the lovely dresses. Madeline cringed; *Oh no, the monthly expense report is becoming more onerous by the minute!* She thought ambivalently as she stared at the extravagant dresses. Jamie's mood was better, but the expense report would be worse. Madeline had to admit Cassone's outfits were beautiful indeed! She wished she could afford even one. *Well maybe I could afford one – if it hadn't taken Jamie fifteen months to get my raise approved. Asking for that raise was worse than having teeth pulled,* she thought. She recalled the day she asked why it was taking so long. It was just the two of them. Jamie was seated at her desk and initially in a good mood which quickly vanished as she whipped herself into a volatile frenzy, raising her voice and stomping her feet in anger. Then a minute or so later she was back to her calm, soft-spoken reserved self. It was embarrassing and surreal indeed, like something out of a Jekyll and Hyde scene.

But on this day, with Vosco Cassone's designer dresses all around, the first lady wore a smile.

"Hello Madeline." Finally Jamie acknowledged her the second time back in the room.

"Good morning, don't forget your appointment with the new hair stylist is at 1 o'clock this afternoon," she said.

"Yes, yes. Tell them I might be running a little late, please."

"I'll call and let them know." Heading back to her small desk Madeline thought cynically to herself, *she'll be late again.*

Madeline had just arranged for a new hair stylist. The old one quit. He explained to Madeline that he could no longer retain the First Lady as a client because every week he and his most valuable assistant were forced to wait around for several hours until she was finally ready. In the beginning he was accommodating, granting her the benefit of the doubt thinking that once or even twice this could happen given the busy schedule of a First Lady. But after experiencing consistent tardiness he soon learned that it was more than just a matter of scheduling. The days spent away from his salon, doing house calls at the

White House, caused him to lose business from some of his best customers – women who would be in town long after the next election.

Back in the Queen's Sitting Room, the chaos continued until finally Jamie emerged in a powder blue evening gown. This was it! Cassone saw what he wanted. For a moment everything stopped. Everyone in the room noticed it. A thousand points of light shone on Jamie Kelly as she stood in splendor before the mirror. It was a Mona Lisa moment. The magnificent blue strapless dress smiled back, paying homage to its new owner. It was perfect for her hair and skin color. Her dark hair and wide set eyes made the dress. Vosco Cassone sighed in captivated approval as the first lady stood before him. In the White House with Mrs. Jamie Kelly, he was designing more than dresses; he was designing an icon - Jamie Kelly! Like no other, the slim brunette beauty possessed a magnetic attractive mystique. Mysterious and ravishing, she had real star power. In Cassone's creations she looked classically beautiful and yet completely new. Together Cassone and Jamie Kelly would make history.

Then as quickly as the magic moment came, it vanished. Jamie reached awkwardly behind and unzipped the dress as she grabbed a package of Salem cigarettes off the fireplace mantle. In her breathy baby voice said, "I'll take it, Vosco. Now let's get a drink!" She stepped into an easy linen chemise and left the room with Vosco, leaving Maria and Vosco's assistant to straighten up in the wake of Hurricane Jamie.

Assassination Point Blank

Chapter 7

Trouble in Paradise

Ellen Lakeland's office window overlooked the Rose Garden. From a good distance she could see President Kelly making his way toward his office. Momentarily she thought about how, in the early months of the administration, Vice President Lionel Jones had made it a habit each morning to take that path through the rose garden on his way to cabinet meetings. The long route brought him through her office and the rooms where the White House press corps congregated. She knew Jones did this to foster the illusion that he and President Kelly had a close, favorable relationship. The reality, Ellen Lakeland knew, was much different. President Kelly had confided in her that when he ran for his next term he would not keep Lionel Jones on the ticket. He had his eye on another Southern Democrat, the governor of North Carolina, with whom he felt he had more in common. The man also had far less baggage.

As President Kelly approached, Ellen retrieved his schedule for the day ahead.

"Good morning, Ellen," the president said, smiling as he came through her office doorway. When he was in town it was his routine at the beginning of each day to be reminded of his schedule.

"Good Morning Mr. President. I have your schedule for today." She handed the paper to Kelly.

Kelly scanned the list.

"Very good, thank you." It was a fairly typical day. He was scheduled to meet in the oval office with his Secretary of State, and then later with the Secretary of the Treasury. Also on the day's schedule was a meeting with his wife's secretary Madeline Murphy. It was an unwelcome break in the routine. "Hopefully Mrs. Murphy will have some good news for once," he remarked.

Later that morning, after finishing his appointments with his Secretary of State and the Secretary of the Treasury, Kelly stood by Ellen's desk. Before heading back to his office, he remained to tell a rather curious joke.

"Ellen, I heard a funny joke yesterday."

"Is that right? Let's hear it."

"A young boy questioned his father, 'Dad is it true that in some countries in the world a man doesn't know his wife until he marries her?'

'No, son,' replied the father. 'That's true in every country.'"

Ellen laughed. It was funny but she couldn't miss the ring of familiarity in it.

***

That afternoon, the president returned from lunch and was in Ellen's office asking her a question when Madeline Murphy arrived for her appointment.

Assassination Point Blank

"Good afternoon Mr. President. Hi Ellen," Madeline said cheerfully as she entered the room.

"Hi Madeline, are you ready to get down to business?" the President asked. "I hope you have some good news for me," he said with a smile.

Madeline was fond of both the President and Ellen. She had worked as a secretary for the Kelly family, including Jamie's mother, for over a decade and was privy to an abundance of personal information about the entire family. Nevertheless, she disliked being stuck as the intermediary between the first lady and the president on matters they couldn't reconcile. There were some things, frankly, that she would rather not know.

"I have the monthly report for you, Mr. President. It's all itemized, as usual, with the canceled checks," Madeline replied as she handed Kelly the black-leather three-ring binder that told all.

"Very good, let's have a look," he said.

At that moment, Madeline recalled her first encounter with the ugly discord regarding Jamie Kelly's spending habits. It occurred while the President was still a senator, on a day he happened to be home from work with a toothache. As she passed his bedroom he said hello and called her in to ask how she was doing. Madeline was pregnant and showing, and he was clearly concerned about her. A few hours later, the President came into the study where Madeline was working; they were making small talk when he noticed a stack of checks on her desk, waiting for Jamie's signature. He immediately started to study the checks more closely and began to question the expenses. In obvious disgust he said in a polite yet firm voice, "Madeline, from now on please give me a list each month detailing every check written and the reason."

The toothache day, Madeline named it because that day was the inception of an ongoing cause of agony, *for her*. The President's attempt to rein in his wife's spending seemed to mark the transition from a distant marriage to overt bad blood between the couple, and Madeline was right in the middle. Now her role was more akin to a referee, although the combatants were not always in the same room.

Madeline considered it a shame that her relationship with the President had to be strained by Jamie's impulsive consumerism. Besides splurging on her wardrobe, Jamie was constantly rearranging the décor, whether it was redecorating their home in Georgetown or the White House. It seemed to Madeline that President Kelly was a simple man and only wanted two things: a quiet place to read, and not to be stressed about money. Jamie made both elusive.

President Kelly's voice brought Madeline back to the present.

"Madeline, it doesn't appear that the figures have gotten any better since last month

- or even the month before, for that matter," he said, flipping through the papers. "In fact, it's continually worse. Did you and Jamie discuss what expenditures could be cut?" the President queried.

"Jamie had some ideas on how to save money, but I told her that they would not be significant without cutting the clothing expenses, which is still by far the largest category."

"What were some of her suggestions?" he inquired.

Madeline didn't know if she should tell the president about all of his wife's "creative ideas" on how to cut expenses.

"Well, since liquor was the second biggest category, she recommended curtailing the drinks at social gatherings."

The president gave a look of disbelief and replied, "Some people like to have a few cocktails. We can't tell people how much to drink. How would the idea work? Our guests would run a private tab at the bar? Or are we going to tell people they can only have one glass of champagne on New Year's Eve?"

Madeline was beginning to sink in her chair.

"And that was her best idea," she sighed.

She certainly did not want to mention some of the others. One was to give the children gifts that were sent to the White House by admirers, instead of buying them herself. Madeline pointed out the problem with that idea, besides the fact that it was ridiculous and wouldn't save much, was that customarily such gifts were given to charity.

Jamie also suggested that the president's aides ask for liquor as gifts, which in turn they would serve at parties. Madeline had to refrain from laughing. Such circumstances would be funny, except that it was her problem too.

Kelly could tell that Madeline had more to say but wasn't.

"What else, Madeline? You have something on your mind, what is it?" he asked.

Madeline didn't quite know how to respond. Jamie was never easy to work for, but lately she seemed positively erratic. She could swing from one mood to another in an instant. She could go from warm and friendly to icy cold in the blink of an eye, as if someone had flipped a switch. Such turbulent mood swings were hard on her staff, and certainly made matters difficult for James Kelly. But now she was being stubborn, or something was genuinely wrong.

"I don't know how to say this, Mr. President. Every time Jamie and I sit down with the books, we have the same conversation. She asks me, 'where do you think we should begin?' and I always tell her, *clothing*. With all due respect Mr. President, it's very redundant. Each month it's as if we've never discussed it," Madeline looked at the President, bewildered.

President Kelly nodded, but didn't speak.

"Is it forgetfulness?" inquired Madeline. Kelly still had no reply. Madeline continued, "I don't think she is purposely asking the same question…"

"I'm not sure whether it's a matter of not listening, not remembering, or something else," the president mused. "Madeline, do you know how to entertain a goldfish?"

"I don't think so," she answered not quite sure where the president was going with his question. His sense of humor sometimes caught people off guard, especially when it came in the middle of a serious discussion.

"A goldfish only remembers a few seconds at a time. So if you put a little castle in its bowl, each time around the bowl it thinks it's seeing something new. Every time it's a surprise."

"I see." Madeline nodded not knowing if she should laugh.

"I'm telling a joke Madeline, but I'm being serious at the same time. The reason I say this is because at times I've noticed in my wife precisely what you've described. I don't know if she does these things intentionally, but it is frustrating. At any rate, I agree with you that clothing expenses are what need to be cut most."

The excesses had been out of control for years. Eventually even a tolerant James Kelly could no longer acquiesce. In 1961, their first year in the White House, Jamie's household spending had exceeded $105,000. The second year it was worse – greater than $121,000! It was astonishing to Madeline that the first lady could manage to spend more than the President's $100,000 salary.

The President understood that what was considered sophisticated and classy today might be perceived as greedy, wasteful and out of touch tomorrow. Moral beliefs about money aside, the President had good political reasons to curtail his wife's reckless behavior. But for the time being at least, Jamie Kelly still held the American public spellbound, letting them see only what she wanted them to see.

Jamie Kelly didn't view money the same way as her husband. By achieving a reputation as the queen of fashion she gained notoriety and admiration, like the royalty of Europe. This was power. By appearing before the public as the perfect wife and companion she was in turn raising her husband's image, albeit in a manner he detested. Madeline was one of the few who knew the couple had been sleeping in separate bedrooms.

Fortunately for the president, his wife was beloved by the media. For some reason the press focused on the first lady's sense of style and fashion without seeming to notice that beauty had a price – in money and in temperament. However, Madeline could recall one exception: a story broke that the First Lady's clothing expenditures had topped $30,000 last year. When she read the story Jamie was outraged. She exclaimed, "Madeline, I would have to wear sable underwear to spend that much on clothes!"

In fact, the journalist was mistaken. Madeline knew the real figure was over $40,000.

At the end of the day, what was being discussed was a divergent view of money. The President and his wife had very different perspectives. For him, money was a tool that could aid in achieving a virtuous goal. It was to be used with wisdom and modesty. Frivolous spending was almost immoral, especially if it was on ephemera that quickly became worthless. For her, she was deserving of the best money could buy.

Chapter 8

Dinner and a Show

Grant Vadala sat at his favorite table in a dim midtown haunt, dining expensively and slowly with a group of friends. Grant was a writer of plays, screenplays, novels, and essays. In the world of film, TV and literature he was well known. Now he was increasingly recognized for a most insulting reason.

"So what is it like being Jamie Kelly's stepbrother?" inquired the young blonde accompanying his friend Michael. *Such a curious question,* thought Grant Vadala. *She should ask Jamie what it was like to be my stepsister!* He was a famous author and intellectual years before anyone even knew the name Jamie Kelly! In fact, over the years he had introduced Jamie to many important people – before she outdid them all. He felt an urge to answer the young lady's question with a scathing retort, but he refrained.

Instead, he answered calmly with a smile reserved for children and dogs. "Your name is Martha, right?" The wide-eyed blonde nodded. Grant would forget her name almost immediately. "Well Martha, I am a few years older than Jamie. At one point my mother married a man called Herman. They divorced and the next year Herman married Jamie's mother. I suppose the fact that we share a stepfather would make us relations, in the eyes of some observers."

He vehemently abhorred Jamie's mother, Janice, and had no qualms about presenting her as a homewrecker. In reality, his mother had left the portly Herman for another man; the marriage had been an outright failure from the beginning. Still he despised Janice. Everything about her he held in contempt, from her cold, dark eyes to her cawing voice that reminded him of an old crow. He found Janice a gold digger of the highest order – and believed she had trained her daughters splendidly in the family trade.

"Do you know Jamie well? Are the two of you close?" continued the young woman innocently, obviously interested in Jamie because of her fashion and celebrity status.

"I was at her wedding to James Kelly, my dear!" replied Grant, a little too loudly. The others at the table were used to his dry sarcasm. It was a pity that Martha missed his tone entirely.

He thoroughly disapproved of Jamie and her sister Leslie. He perceived them as phonies, shallow and deceitful. But he did admit to himself that they certainly had the majority fooled - including this young lady. As much as he hated to concede them any skill whatsoever, they were fine actresses. And the entire world was a stage.

"In her youth," Grant smiled, "Jamie wanted to be an actress; I introduced her to some people I thought would be helpful." Grant was gentlemanly enough to leave out the fact that Jamie could prove impulsive and even reckless at times, and had made the acquaintance of a number of gentlemen in the process. He had been told by a friend that she gave up her virginity in a Paris hotel elevator to a man who was later known best as a founding writer for the CIA bankrolled *Paris Review.* Her junior year of college she spent in France. It was a busy year, Grant learned. She was romanced by writer Armand de Lay. She fell in love with a mysterious government official. She had a crush on an aristocrat and dated the son of a French diplomat.

There were other more interesting stories. Grant discovered that after graduating from college in 1951, Jamie asked her stepfather's good friend, CIA director Albert Diller, for assistance in obtaining an entry level position at the CIA. The agency was recruiting on college campuses, especially the Ivy Leagues as well as the Seven Sisters, a group of women's colleges including Smith and Vassar. Both institutions were sister schools to Yale. She was admitted to a special job on a certain project. Jamie's first employer didn't surprise Grant. Herman and Janice had many friends in the intelligence community. Herman's son from his first marriage worked for the CIA.

Grant had long enjoyed the luxury of knowing more than ordinary people about the doings of extraordinary folk. Jamie's dalliances and espionage work were his secret, and he found media representations of the

President as lothario and Jamie as long-suffering wife to be hilarious. He knew that appearances and reality were far different.

"So your mother and Jamie's mother were married to the same man, but you have different mothers and fathers?" The young lady persisted, baffled by the connection.

"Herman, the gentleman in question, in fact married three times – and he remains ever hopeful. He had one son from his first marriage, another two with my mother and two more with Jamie's mother. And of course through marriage he acquired stepchildren, including me, Jamie and her sister, Princess Leslie. And that's the story," Grant finished bitterly, hoping the subject would drop.

"Was her biological father still alive for all this?" inquired Michael, scandalized.

"Oh, indeed! He passed away only about five or six years ago. Unfortunately, from what I hear, he was a man of addictions. It didn't come as a surprise to me that he engaged in such naughty behavior though, being married to Janice. Tragic really. He loved to gamble and drink. His brother was a heavy drinker too and unfortunately died at an early age."

"That would be Jamie's uncle." Michael said looking at Martha, whose expression had now become more serious. Obviously her idealistic image of Jamie Bene Kelly had been shaken. Unlike most Americans she was able to get a rare peak behind the curtain at the First Lady. Not liking the view, she decided at last, to change the subject. Michael hoped their evening might still be rescued.

"What about the president? What do you think of him?" She said changing the subject but not enough.

"He's one of the worst presidents we've had in a long time," snapped a still irritated Grant.

"Why is that?"

"Every operation he's undertaken, my dear, has been a disaster. That's why! First there was the debacle with the invasion of Cuba. And the way he handled the negotiations with Khrushchev has completely antagonized the Soviets. I'll say he's one of the most charming and charismatic men I've ever had the pleasure to meet, and yet I hate to admit he is dreadful at his job." Grant thought to himself that he had said enough. He didn't enjoy criticizing President Kelly because of his fondness for the man, but it couldn't really be helped.

Grant's brutally frank responses were startling. Martha finally relented. Grant's dose of reality brought any lofty idealism of the Kelly's back down to earth. Fortunately, Martha could tell by the look on Michael's face that Grant was ok with her, just not talking about the Kelly's, especially Jamie. The conversation at the table moved on to Broadway, literature and other interests. After coffee and dessert the group of friends departed the restaurant.

Chapter 9

The Statesman and his Joint Chiefs of Staff

President Kelly looked across the massive Pentagon conference table, listening patiently to his military advisors' suggestions regarding the instability in Southeast Asia. About a year earlier he brought Army General Tyler out of retirement to become the new Chairman of the Joint Chiefs of Staff. It was an abrupt change in military and political strategy. General Tyler, unlike his predecessor, Symon Semnitzer, believed that it was possible that U.S. combat troops would not be required to prevent communism from taking over Southeast Asia. However, the government of South Vietnam was unstable and getting worse.

One weekend in late August 1963, while the President the Secretary of Defense McNeil and the Director of the CIA were out of town, a mysterious telegram had been sent from the State Department in Washington to the US ambassador in South Vietnam. In the Pentagon they called it Cable 243. In the White House they called it insubordination. It was an unauthorized communication sent by rogue members of the State Department – but once sent, it could not really be retracted.

Cable 243 threatened that Washington would no longer support President Diem of South Vietnam unless he agreed to remove his brother from power, an act they knew he would refuse. His younger brother was his political advisor but held no official title, making the request nearly impossible. Even more damaging, the cable also encouraged a coup by stating that the United States would support the military leaders in an uprising if one should occur.

The President and Attorney General were outraged when they came back from a weekend away to find that the Under Secretary of State for Political Affairs, Avery Harrison's department, was responsible for sending the cable. The movers and shakers in the East Coast Establishment wanted South Vietnamese President Diem out of office. Kelly was appalled that people in the State Department would usurp his authority and send the telegram without approval. The administration had placed great trust in Harrison to oversee this faction. He had failed them.

Now President Kelly and his advisors were gathered to discuss the status of Vietnam and Cable 243. After the Secretary of Defense Roderick McNeil's opening remarks concerning the situation, Chairman Tyler spoke first. "Mr. President, militarily the situation is still positive but the survival capacity of the government of South Vietnam is deteriorating." The Chairman paused. "The telegram sent to the Ambassador was damaging." The administration had considered rescinding the telegram, but decided against it as did the Joint Chiefs. Once it was sent it created a no-win situation. They were stuck with the strong possibility of a coup in South Vietnam, and now they had to figure out what to do about it. Rogue elements in the State Department hoped it would lead to war.

"The telegram was a grave mistake," President Kelly began. He moved his eyes from one advisor to the next. "It has made a bad situation worse. Nevertheless we have to stay focused so that our military advisors in Asia continue to make progress." The President tried to stay optimistic, but he knew that the telegram was catastrophic to Washington's relationship with Diem. Relations were fragile even before the incident. He couldn't believe what had transpired. To act as a renegade and encourage the overthrow of a leader of a sovereign country was unthinkable. Diem's regime was unstable but he was willing to work with Washington and the North Vietnamese for a peaceful solution.

"We will do our best, Mr. President. In light of the new developments now undermining Diem, it would be prudent to make a detailed contingency plan in case he is removed," General Tyler reiterated in his cool even tone.

"Mr. President, I agree with Chairman Tyler. There is now a greater chance that the Generals will move against President Diem if they believe his removal is to their advantage," Admiral Adams, the Chief of Naval Operations added. "So even if Diem stays in power it will make our job more difficult going forward. Like you Mr. President, I want to see a diplomatic solution, but that telegram is worrisome," he concluded with a concerned look.

Briefing files were stacked before the President. The brief on top of the stack had a map of Southeast Asia on the cover. He scanned through one or two briefs he hadn't seen before, and turned his gaze to the Admiral, "We can still settle this with diplomacy." Kelly was still confident that if Diem remained in office they could work together for a peaceful resolution. Secretly his inner circle was making progress with Castro, even after two humiliating debacles in Cuba. But no one in this room knew about those talks, so his optimism at negotiation in Vietnam seemed naïve.

The president and his Joint Chiefs spent the afternoon discussing Southeast Asia including Vietnam, Laos, and Thailand. Afterward, as he addressed the entire room in a relaxed yet serious tone, Kelly said confidently, "We need to learn from our mistakes. After giving consideration to all your information and ideas I've decided what we're going to do regarding this conflict. For the time being, we will continue to train our allies and monitor the situation. We will settle all of these problems the same way as the nuclear arms race – with diplomacy. I appreciate all your ideas and expertise and look forward to our next meeting." The men all stood and saluted President Kelly.

The President was resolute. He came prepared, had given considerable thought to all the options, and had made his decision. He would remain steadfast on finding a diplomatic solution.

Chapter 10

Enemies Within

President Kelly sat down in his office with his brother, noticing the angle of the afternoon sun's rays flatten inexorably in the oval room as the sun descended on the horizon.

"How did it go yesterday with the Joint Chiefs?" the Attorney General inquired as he stood in front of the large desk with his hands on his hips.

"The Joint Chiefs went as expected. It's the State Department that has me concerned, but you already knew that. I think we have the Joint Chiefs on the same page with us, at least for now."

"After Operation Northwoods, I didn't think it could get any worse," replied Scott with bitterness only the President could fully appreciate. The previous year, the entire Joint Chiefs of Staff signed off on a proposal known as Operation Northwoods. The proposal called for the CIA or other intelligence operatives to commit acts of terrorism in U.S. cities, on airplanes or ships and blame it on Cuba. This would serve as a pretext to invade the island. It was the brainchild of the CIA and hawkish military men including the Chairman of the Joint Chiefs of Staff at the time, Symon Semnitzer. President Kelly was flabbergasted and sickened that there would be consensus on such a reckless plan. He rejected the treacherous operation and spent the next several months replacing members of the Joint Chiefs. The changes were barely covered in the press, but the military and intelligence communities certainly got the message.

"So what did they have to say?"

"They said even though our advisors have made good progress in training the South Vietnamese army, it would now be more difficult going forward. The cable encouraged a *coup d'état*, and that seems more likely now."

"What was your reply?"

"I told them that I understand their new challenge but that if it comes to an all out war with U.S. combat troops the communists can outnumber us 5-1 or better, which they already know."

"Like in Korea," the Attorney General said as he pulled up a chair and sat down.

"Yes," the president replied. "And what would be our end game? When do we leave, if we go in with troops? Plus, is it even constitutional? I repeated all the points I've made in the past. They understood. They're just frustrated, and so am I."

"And with our friends in the press, they'll play the same old game," Scott Kelly said sarcastically. "If we don't go in with troops we're soft on communism." Scott Kelly looked at the ceiling. "We made changes in the CIA and the Joint Chiefs, and now it looks like we have to clean out the State Department too? Isn't Avery watching over these people?" Scott Kelly was always fond of Harrison. There must be some explanation.

The President turned to his brother. "Like his friends, he wants Diem out too. He's been advising presidents for so long he figures he knows best. Like Jones, sometimes he acts as if he forgot he is not the president."

"Avery is a good guy, and I know he wants the best for our country, but I can't believe he'd look the other way. This is a serious problem. In either case, the government is broken in two." There was one faction of the government in favor of war versus the Kelly brothers and their loyal friends advocating diplomacy. They had come against the east coast elite. Harrison was their advocate to bridge the gaps and for some reason he wasn't doing the job.

"That's what we're going to have to do," the president said while staring out the window.

"What?"

"Clean house. When I'm re-elected we're going to make more moves, even bigger ones. Maybe more changes on the Joint Chiefs again. And as far as I'm concerned the CIA is done. That's it for them. Instead of gathering intelligence they're stirring things up in Vietnam. In my next term, all its operations will fall under the military and FBI. And Lionel Jones is finished too, along with all his corruption down in Texas. I'll get a new running mate."

"And Harvey Hampton too, right?"

"Yes, after the election he's gone. He's going to have to retire. He's been in power running the FBI longer than most dictators." The men laughed.

"When I took this job, I didn't realize that in the process of putting America first, we would have to step on *this* many toes." It was true. In the process, they had become surrounded by enemies; enemies who were increasingly uncontrollable and unaccountable.

As he rose from his desk President Kelly looked at his watch. "So many problems, and so little time," he said philosophically as the two brothers slowly made their way to dinner.

Chapter 11

The Secret Brotherhood & the New World Order

It was a meeting of the wise men, the great benefactors of society, men specially endowed to rule. As the elder spoke, the aroma of his pipe tobacco permeated the room. "During World War II we discovered the Japanese war plunder hidden in the Philippines. The treasure was acquired by their military during its imperial expansion and conquest of the countries in Southeast Asia. When the United States won the naval battles at Midway and the Coral Sea, the Japanese Navy's safe passage back to their homeland was cutoff. For Japan, it was more than just a military defeat. They were unable to take their gold and precious gems back to the Land of the Rising Sun. As a solution, the emperor resorted to a secondary plan and formed Operation Golden Lily in which a few of his most trusted military men hid the treasure in various caves in the Philippines, thinking they could quietly return for it after the war. That way, even if they lost the war militarily, they still stood to benefit financially. Fortunately, one of our own in the Secret Brotherhood got there first, after he received word of a hidden cache in a cave on the northern island of Luzon. It led to more."

Like the Cheshire cat in *Alice and Wonderland,* Albert Diller wore a mischievous grin. The ubiquitous Secret Brotherhood had hit the mother load of the Pacific theatre. Guthrie Buscher sat captivated. The organization's former director continued to explain the mysterious history of the CIA and how it acquired its incredible power two decades earlier, while still known as the Office of Strategic Services (OSS).

"That's a sample from Java. We found it hidden in a cave in Luzon," said Preston Buscher, Guthrie's father, who was sitting to his right as he pointed in the direction of a beautiful gold Buddha inside a glass display case.

Diller nodded and continued, "For obvious reasons we kept our discovery confidential, even from officials in Washington. And with our Black Eagle Fund we have progressed faster than we could ever have imagined. Our friend Jay McClare was instrumental in getting the trust accounts set up with the backing of the gold." JJ McClare was the President of the World Bank, the powerful chairman of the CFR and close confidant to all the men in the room. Diller laughed, "The emperor was more than willing to throw his General Yamashita under the bus as a war criminal to save himself and do business with us." Guthrie understood that members of the Brotherhood effectively took over the Bank of Japan after the war and that some trust accounts were set up in Japanese banks. President Truman likely received a cut and had the atomic bomb at his fingertips causing the emperor to think twice about reneging.

Diller peered over his round glasses at Guthrie. "And I'd just like to digress for a moment to say that you've done a very fine job for us Guthrie. We've been impressed by you, ever since your accomplishments serving as a Navy pilot in the Pacific theatre. Your day is coming." Smoke from Diller's pipe spiraled slowly toward the dimly lit ceiling lights.

Another man in the room in obvious agreement with Diller was the CIA's Bob Angler. Angler was narrow-faced and wore heavy black rimmed glasses. Both his face and body resembled a skeleton. He was also a member of Skull and Bones. Angler nodded with approval at the older man's praise. Diller was an important part of the Secret Brotherhood and the former head of the CIA. *There was no doubt from the body language and dialogue in the room that Diller was still a force to be reckoned with and continued to run operations from behind the scenes through Bob Angler,* thought Guthrie. It was no secret that Albert Diller clung to a righteous indignation over being fired from the CIA, and he was hell bent on getting even.

"Our operations haven't worked out as expected in Cuba, but your company proved instrumental," Diller continued. Indeed, Guthrie's organization had helped train rebels in Florida for the invasion and his oil company acted as a front for espionage activity and gun running. Diller and Angler were acknowledging their appreciation. That was big.

Assassination Point Blank

Speaking of their secret society's oaths, Angler turned to Guthrie. "Success is assured," he said confidently. "And keep in mind, as Patriarchs of The Order we have the special cable tow of camaraderie." Guthrie and Angler were members of the same exclusive secret society at Yale known as the Order of Skull and Bones. Guthrie's father Preston and his powerful business partner, the Old Crocodile, Avery Harrison were also members, as was the current National Security Advisor. The Order was one of the most elite secret societies within the larger Secret Brotherhood pyramid. Diller's presence and Angler's confidence meant that multiple secret societies and intelligence organizations were working together in agreement to achieve the same goal. Being the top representatives of banking, politics and industry, these men *were* the East Coast Establishment and could move in any society they chose. Hidden behind the curtain of secrecy they were accustomed to having their hands on the levers of power. Angler stared at the grandfather clock in the room. Finally Guthrie's eyes looked in that direction. "Remember Guthrie," Angler explained, "Presidents come and go, but the Order is eternal."

He felt a sense of thrill. The wise men had groomed him. He was held in high esteem and when the changing of the old guard occurred, he would one day become the top Patriarch of The Order. It was the ultimate vote of confidence. He saw the prideful expression on his father's face. A sense of excitement and expectation rushed through his body while he was being praised and promoted by some of the most powerful men in the world, his mentors.

He was familiar with the network's large slush funds. Funds used to finance covert black ops - operations which could not be proposed publicly in Washington. However, up until now he had never heard the entire tale of the Brotherhood's Asian treasure. It fascinated him. Power came from the barrel of a gun the communists liked to say. That was true; but it also came from teamwork, inside information and wealth. Fifteen men marching together were far more powerful than a thousand walking to their own beat. Thanks to their intelligence operations, growing revenue streams and treasure, the Secret Brotherhood had it all. In less than 20 years after the discovery of the treasure the CIA had made great progress. Alliances were made with other intelligence agencies around the world such as the British MI-6, the Mossad, and the SDECE of France were cemented. Greek shipping families, international bankers, and organized crime were also partners included in money making enterprises such as the proliferation of narcotics. In less than two decades they became a major force in the world. Finally, they could see their utopia coming into view. Protected behind a veil of secrecy, aided by their massive treasure and a new cash flow from their illegal drug business, the CIA evolved into a fifth column, corrupting and overthrowing legitimate governments. It was only one of the organizations the Brotherhood had infiltrated.

With growing resources they were usurping the government and media of the United States, placing fellow members in positions of power. In the same way the KGB was operating in the Soviet Union, they were maneuvering in the United States, only with higher sophistication and stealth. They would be able to work with the corrupt Lionel Jones once he came to power and in time they would place one of their own in the White House.

Guthrie's father had participated in a failed coup years earlier, when FDR was president. They survived, and even made money off the war by trading with the enemy. After the war, Avery Harrison became instrumental in the secret buildup of the Soviet Union. A new foe was needed. Conflict created more money making opportunities, this time in the form of the Cold War. The coup in the 30s didn't work out exactly as planned but they learned from their mistakes. The power of the intelligence agencies in the three decades since 1933 had grown exponentially, and the Secret Brotherhood were founders and insiders in these organizations. This time they would leave nothing to chance. Kelly, unlike FDR, was stubborn and unwilling to get with the program. It was impossible for them to work with such a man.

"The Brotherhood has been around for centuries and we always have a way to solve our problems, including this one," Albert Diller explained as he tapped his pipe on the side of the large ceramic ash tray sitting next to his chair.

"I'll help anyway I can," Guthrie answered with bold enthusiasm. He had no apprehension. He was confident he would live to see the Secret Brotherhood's creation of a New World Order, where the entire planet would be governed by a One World rule of law, not the law of the jungle. He was their rising star, from a desirable pedigree. He had reason to be confident. The Brotherhood had infiltrated deep into the Kelly administration. They had other secret society members working toward the same goal. James Kelly's brother-in-law, Sevin Scheyer, was a member of Scroll and Key, another secret society at Yale working for the Brotherhood's greater good. Guthrie heard that Scheyer was a good source of information and would be rewarded once the great work was completed.

Decades earlier, Guthrie's father had become legendary in the Brotherhood when he and five others dug up and stole the skull of a famous Apache warrior from an Oklahoma reservation. They brought it back to The Order's tomb in Connecticut. The warrior and his tribe had been one of the last holdouts against imperial expansion in the late 1800s. The desecration was not a prank or hazing conducted by some small-minded and misguided fraternity boys. It was symbolic and tapped into occult power. Guthrie knew the meaning. Any man who opposed the Secret Brotherhood would have his head handed to him. Nobody would be allowed to resist their plan. Even the wealthy, charismatic James Kelly would soon meet the same fate as the Apache.

Angler interrupted his thoughts. "The old leadership in South Vietnam will soon be gone," he said with a smug look on his skeleton like face. "And with such change comes an opportunity for windfall profits." If necessary, through assassination the CIA would remove the Vietnamese leader and his brother from power. It would then be open season in the Golden Triangle. "We are getting closer to our goal. The poppy fields of Southeast Asia are gold mines," Angler said, referring to the opium producing poppies and the heroin drug trade. "But this president is determined to hold us back." Guthrie knew a war in Vietnam, if it came, would be more than a battle of communism against capitalism. Behind the scenes it would be a drug war, and very profitable for the Secret Brotherhood.

Unaccountable to leaders or the citizenry, the secret societies and the intelligence organizations they had infiltrated, they had become a shadow force in world governments. In achieving their goals, they believed in the Hegelian dialectic and the axioms: *Might is right.'* *'If you have the power, use it to achieve the objectives of the Brotherhood'* and finally, *'Do what thou wilt,'* as long as it meets the Brotherhood's objectives. War and opium in Southeast Asia were big businesses. They would not allow any man to block their plans. In a few weeks, there would be no more delay.

As the men stood up to leave, Guthrie shook hands with the patriarchs. Even the subtleness of their handshakes contained secret information concealed from the ignorant masses. He studied a plaque on the wall. He recognized the epigram from their The Order. The plaque had a picture of four human skulls lying together. Above them in German was inscribed:

Wer war der Thor, wer Weiser, Bettler oder Kaiser?

The translation: "Which one was the wise man, the fool, the beggar or the king?"

And below the skulls was the Brotherhood's answer:

Ob Arm, ob Reich, im Tode gleich.

"Whether poor or rich they are the same in death."

It was a macabre reminder for all the members of The Order to give their utmost effort in achieving the Secret Brotherhood's secular goals.

Guthrie pondered a moment. In his secret society also known as The Order, each year fifteen new members were required to receive an initiation. During the ritual they would lie inside a casket in a dark section of the tomb and reveal their innermost secrets to the group, after which the initiate received a new name. Often times it was a mythological, occult, or nefarious biblical name. They were taught that they were reborn into The Order after rising back out of the coffin. It was their version of Christianity's spiritual regeneration known as being born again. Many prominent men had gone through the ritual including his father's business partner, the great Avery Harrison, and the founder of Time magazine Hayden Lucy. While closely adhering to the plaque's message instructing members to do the utmost here on earth, most members still believed in a powerful force, known by many names including the Light-bearer, Son of the Morning, the Architect of the Universe, just to mention a few, who was guiding their glorious plan here on earth. Through ritual, they could conjure this hidden power which would assist them in their work.

But regardless whether an individual member was an atheist or if he experienced the guiding force of the Light-bearer, we all share the same earthly goal, mused a grinning Guthrie.

Chapter 12

Taking Care of Business

Vice President Lionel Jones knew how to handle knotty problems. By 1963 scandals were building and he realized if something wasn't done his days in politics could be over. For guidance, he drew from his previous successes in solving controversies. In his political career he survived numerous scandals, including a fraudulent vote counting episode in Texas that allowed him to win his Senate seat in 1948. He won by the narrowest of margins, less than 100 votes. Ballots were burned and one election boss was later found murdered. But from that sordid beginning Lionel rose to become the most powerful man in the U.S. Senate. Along the way he befriended oil tycoons, businessmen and other politicians who helped his career. Mutual back scratching was necessary in Texas and Lionel was frequently asked for favors. He acquired a reputation of a man willing to do anything if the price was right. Typically that price was 10% - in cash.

Over the years Lionel had learned to first use finesse in resolving his troubles. However, if that failed he would not hesitate to act in a more expedient manner. Being ruthless, he buried the scandals and corruption he created. His illegitimate children he skillfully kept private, working through intermediaries to support his mistresses financially.

On one such occasion, in June of 1961, he faced a problem which could not be negotiated. His difficulty was with a U.S. Agriculture official. The man, Harry Miller, snooped around too far and uncovered illegal Texas cotton allotment purchases and a fertilizer scheme run by one of Lionel's business partners. Following the paper trail like a bloodhound, Miller had reached the partner and if unchecked he would have been sniffing around near Lionel's doorstep. And there was no way that was going to happen.

If pursued, the investigation would have certainly led to him. At first he and his friends tried to finesse Miller into letting the matter slide, but Miller was an individual of impeccable character and could not be bribed, nor could the matter be covered up. As a sophisticated bribe attempt Miller was offered a promotion which would lead to his transfer out of West Texas. But Miller, a man of integrity, refused, and Lionel had no choice but to put Harry Miller at the top of Mo Walter's list. In a last ditch effort they tried threats, but Miller was a hard head; he pressed on. The problem had to be handled the old fashioned way. Behind his large desk, Lionel sat back in his chair and relived how he solved the thorny problem by bringing in Clint Carson and Mo Walters as a last resort. He picked up the phone.

***

Assassination Point Blank

It was in early June 1961 when Clint Carson was expecting the call. When it came it was no surprise. He had worked for Lionel Jones for decades, starting in the 1930s as a volunteer. His specialty became mudslinging and the smearing of opponents. After a stint in World War II, he rejoined the Jones team as one of Lionel's most trusted men, so well trusted that he was assigned as a courier of important information, messages, and most importantly money. One rival politician accurately referred to him as Lionel's "bagman," but Carson also made other important arrangements.

"I need something taken care of," began a deep whispering voice with a southern drawl on the opposite end of the phone.

"Alright, when?" replied Carson. It was his boss.

"I need this handled real soon too - as soon as possible. You know the aggie? The one who didn't take the promotion, you know who. It's time" said the voice now sounding like a faint growl.

"Yes I know. I understand. Not a problem, I'll take care of it."

"Good. And after give me a call and we'll arrange a time to meet at the ranch."

"All right," Carson hesitated for a second. He had something on his mind. "Uh, one other thing, when we meet at the ranch, we have to talk about your sister."

"I know what you're going to say. She's talking too much after she's been drink'n," Lionel knew they would have to do something about his out of control sister. He had told his associates to keep a close eye on her and make sure she wasn't running her mouth about his business.

"This can't keep happening."

"I know. First things first, we'll discuss it at the ranch."

"All right, I'll call you later."

"Bye..." A click, then the line went dead.

Carson hung up the phone. He understood the instructions to mean that it was now time to call Mo Walters. If Mo Walters could make it look like a suicide that would be best, but if that would prove difficult he was free to take care of it by any means necessary.

After hanging up the phone Carson opened the door and sprang out of the room like a cheetah. He jumped in his car and headed for the familiar pay phone he often used about a mile from his house.

"Hello"

"Mo, it's me. I've got something you need to take care of. And I need you to put it at the top of your list. Can you meet me later today at Harry's Grill?"

"Yeah, sure"

"It's urgent. This is coming from up top, from you know who."

"No big deal. How about we meet at 1?"

"Fine, see you then."

"Bye."

Carson hung up the phone. Harry Miller was history. A problem easily swept under the rug, Carson thought.

Chapter 13

The Texas Mafia, June 1961

It was a bright Texas morning. Morris "Mo" Walters had Harry Miller, the man he had been tailing for some time, right where he wanted him. He was stalking his prey for some time. He knew the terrain and exactly when to make his move on a desolate Texas state highway.

This is the spot, he thought. The road curved to the left. Just before Miller's car took the curve and came into a long straightaway Carson gunned the accelerator and swung the work truck into the passing lane, quickly positioning it alongside his victim's smaller car. He already had the passenger side window rolled all the way down and his 12 gauge shotgun ready on the front seat. Thinking the truck was going to pass him, the man initially slowed his car a bit allowing Carson to get along side. But as the hit man's truck made it into the passing lane a gun barrel emerged from the window.

Looking in his driver's side door mirror, Miller spotted Walters' shotgun barrel poking out. He immediately panicked. With a racing heart and bulging eyes he was overcome with horror. Hesitating at first, not knowing whether to hit the breaks or accelerate, he floored the little car hoping he might be able to outrun the truck. But Walters was too quick.

He was right on him. Harry Miller's split second delay was dooming.

Walters put the shotgun bead on his target and blasted away. The second he pulled the trigger the truck bounced a little causing the first shot to be a bit high. It shattered the driver's side window, making holes in the roof and cracking the windshield. Miller's car careened wildly out of control, first swerving onto the shoulder and then whipsawing back onto the road. When the little car screeched back onto the pavement, Walters was ready for it. He turned the heavy truck's steering wheel to the right and smashed the small car back toward the shoulder, causing it to slow on the gravel. He took aim again, this time the shotgun blast entered dead center into the driver's window squarely hitting its target. The little car ran off the road crashing violently into a deep ditch.

It was unlikely anyone could survive two shotgun blasts and such a devastating car accident, but Mo left nothing to chance. He slammed on the brakes, causing skid marks on the pavement as the truck finally came to a halt on the shoulder.

Almost before the truck stopped, Walters had jumped out and was already running toward the little car now in the ditch perhaps fifty yards behind. With the shotgun in one hand and a revolver in a holster he ran along the shoulder. As he approached the car he could see that the front end was badly collapsed as it hit the opposite side of the ditch flipping the vehicle sideways. He peered into the driver's side window. One wheel was still spinning but the inside of the car was motionless. Harry Miller, the agriculture official that had caused Lionel Jones so much consternation, was now dead. Fortunately he was alone in the car. But Mo was not taking any chances. He pumped another round into the window throwing the already bloody body onto the passenger side. All that remained was a mangled, twisted body. Miller's head was mutilated.

Walters ran back to the idling truck, threw it into gear and hit the accelerator. The truck made a high pitched winding noise as it lurched back onto the road. Twisting the steering wheel with both arms he whirled the truck around and was now heading in the opposite direction.

From the time the shooting started the entire incident took less than three minutes. There were no cars or people around, only cotton fields and cattle grazing in a nearby pasture. After about five minutes of silence driving in the opposite direction, Mo began laughing. *He's not going to be talking to any newspaper reporters,* Mo thought. He turned down a desolate dirt road and pulled the blue work truck behind a grove of trees. As he exchanged vehicles he noticed a rattlesnake crossing the road in front of him. He jumped in a black truck and in no time was back on the country road.

After driving through the Texas hill country for about forty-five minutes Walters arrived at a restaurant he often frequented and strolled nonchalantly inside to enjoy some ham, eggs and coffee as if he had just returned from an uneventful morning of skeet shooting. He wasn't worried. He knew the entire event would somehow be explained as an accident or a suicide. He first made a beeline to the pay phone inside the restaurant, which had a privacy door, and dialed. The phone rang a few times. It was a direct line. Finally a man came on the phone. He recognized the voice.

"Hello"

"It's all taken care of"

"Excellent."

"When can you see me?"

"I'm meeting him at the ranch tomorrow afternoon at about four and I'll let him know. After I'm done I'll call you, so I'm thinking maybe tomorrow afternoon or evening."

"Fine, I'll be at home, let me know." Mo hung up the phone. Hopefully Carson would have his money the next evening. He was the go-between for enough of these assignments to know the drill.

***

Lionel's troubles were not confined to his illegitimate children and government officials. Even some of his legitimate relatives such as his sister, Josephine, had caused problems for him. Although they shared many of the same vices, Lionel applied a double standard in dealing with his sister's indiscretions. From his point of view, she partied too much, drank excessively, and had gotten a reputation. When she was drunk she talked too much about his business deals and even became involved with one of his hatchet men, Mo Walters. Like him she engaged in lascivious behavior and after breaking off a short relationship with Mo she started a new one with a handsome golf pro. This sent Walters into a jealous rage. In cold blood he murdered the man in broad daylight inside his golf shop. A disgusted Lionel was forced to call in a favor and have Walters's trial rigged. Through Jones's string pulling, Walters received a suspended sentence. Regrettably, Josephine talked out of turn one too many times and was found dead after returning home from a holiday party at Lionel's ranch in December of 1961. No autopsy was conducted, despite the fact that Josephine was only in her late forties and died of a cerebral hemorrhage. Evidently, Lionel didn't seem to find his sister's suspicious death all that mysterious and didn't insist on an autopsy.

Chapter 14

Mistress Maggie, Summer 1963

"When are you coming out, my Sandow?"

Lying on the four-poster bed in the exquisite hotel suite, Maggie propped her head up on one arm and gazed in the direction of the bathroom. The room's white walls were adorned with ornate crown molding. The ceiling paint matched the color of the dark hardwood floor. Maggie's husband had served in the Pacific during World War II but the brutality of war destroyed his mental faculties, creating a violent drunkard. He eventually was institutionalized with a mental illness. The ravages of war had turned him into a belligerent killing machine; a man who could never separate war from peace. Consequently, the beautiful redhead was forced to count on her resourcefulness and intelligence to survive and raise two children.

Maggie waited. She loved having sex with him. He was large - six feet, four inches tall - and his enormous ego made him concerned about satisfying her. He knew how to excite her erotic zones with passion and skill. She fell for him the moment they met, years ago, while he was still a senator.

As her lover finally opened the bathroom door, his tall naked silhouette stood momentarily in the doorway, behind him was a three way bathroom mirror. "Ready for dessert, my beautiful Texas rose?" he asked. "We have to hurry though; I have to get back to Washington today."

"Lionel, I love you. But you know you are a married man and in the spotlight now. What is our future?"

"Today is today and tomorrow is tomorrow, darling," answered the big Texan. "Worry about the here and now." He pulled her off the bed against his body, kissing her passionately with his tongue, ready to go a second round.

Maggie knew that Lionel loved her, but not as much as she loved him. He had given her a mink coat and a brand new Ford Coupe and from their unholy rendezvous they had a child together, an illegitimate son. Lionel kept his promise to take care of them financially even though he was married. She wanted him to acknowledge her son but she sympathized with his position. It just wasn't possible. It conflicted with his ambitious career goals. She only hoped that perhaps after he retired from politics he would develop a deep and truthful relationship with their son.

Sometimes after their passionate love making he would explain to her how his wife Raven Tyler was unaffectionate. She was a woman only concerned with money and power. Lionel told Maggie his marriage to Raven was one of opportunity. His father suggested he date girls from only the wealthiest families. He could still hear his Dad's voice advising him, 'Let me tell you something, boy. You can make more

money at the altar than in a lifetime of work.'
Being a tall handsome Texan, Lionel took his
old man's advice and after dating several girls
from affluent families he finally married Raven
Tyler, the daughter of the wealthiest man in
the county. Raven was a plain, homely looking
woman. Fitting of her name, her nose was beak-
like. Despite her physical shortcomings, she
was an intelligent, ambitious businesswoman.
Holding tight to the reigns of money, she at
times pushed the lanky Lionel around.
Nevertheless, he was a man on a mission. His
wife's dominant behavior was a motivator for
him. It gave him an obsession with obtaining
his own money and power – and mistresses. After
all, he didn't want to be henpecked. He liked
to screw women and he wouldn't be able to do so
if his wife was the only one in the family
wearing the pants.

As their marriage progressed, the two
reached an understanding. They worked together
when required but had separate lives. Raven was
busy being a mother and running her businesses
including a radio broadcasting company. Lionel
was always working, building his political
power, using it to cut lucrative deals – and
having affairs with pretty ladies on the side.

"Oh, my precious little redheaded lady," he
sighed as he affectionately held Maggie close.
He knew it would be more difficult for them to
get together once he became President. But
power was its own aphrodisiac. *It was a fair
tradeoff,* he thought.

Chapter 15

Dr. Feel Right

Back in the Oval office, seated in a leather chair near the president's desk was the Attorney General. He was in the middle of a discussion with his brother and could detect obvious pain in the President's eyes. Stress was making his back troubles worse. After a few minutes of uncomfortable shuffling about in his chair, James Kelly finally pressed the intercom button and called his secretary.

"Yes, Mr. President."

"Ellen, could you please see if it is possible for Dr. Abramson to come to the office sometime today? My back is acting up again."

"Yes, sir I will call him right away. In the meantime is there anything else I can do?"

"No thanks, Ellen. That will be all." With one hand Ellen hung up the intercom, and with the other picked up her desk phone to call the doctor.

That quack is coming here again, Scott Kelly thought as he pulled back the gray sleeve of his suit jacket to check his watch. Over the previous two and a half years, Abramson had already visited the White House dozens of times. *Clearly the so-called doctor is only treating my brother's symptoms,* Scott thought. Was this an appropriate time to tell his brother what his informants had recently unearthed regarding Dr. Sid Abramson? Abramson was known as Dr. Feel Right because of the miraculous results he obtained for his list of celebrity clients. The nickname stuck because his drug laced injections did indeed relieve pain immediately. But Scott Kelly had gotten word that there was more than just amphetamines and pain killers in the magic formula the quack doctor was using for his medicine cocktails. He was told that the shots had other mysterious ingredients, from monkey glands to steroids. Although he didn't necessarily suspect Dr. Abramson of any intentional maliciousness, he decided he had to warn the President.

"Those shots Abramson is giving you could be dangerous. Not only do they have addictive drugs in them, which I realize you need to alleviate your pain, but they also contain the organs of lab animals. I'm concerned," he said earnestly. Still trying to position himself in his chair, he could see his brother was in intense pain as they exchanged a glance. "Abramson may have left Germany, but he didn't leave their unethical experimental practices behind," continued the Attorney General.

A little irritated, yet still trying to be funny, the President replied, "Scott, I don't care if it's horse piss, it works! He's the only doctor who's been able to help me with my back. He's helped Jamie too."

With such a dismissive reaction Scott knew his brother well enough to recognize that he was not going to change his mind.

"I'm just looking out for you," he replied. Maybe the President was right. Was he being overly paranoid? Despite his suspicions, what he knew thus far was only rumor. He would need to obtain more information, more proof of the ingredients contained in the injections. He dropped the conversation, but further investigation was clearly on his to-do list.

***

Later that day the eccentric Dr. Abramson made his appearance at the White House. A few years earlier the president was given a referral to the doctor from his friend Craig Sperling, a Yale graduate. "An Eli introduced me to my wife and an Eli referred me to Dr. Feel Right," the president joked. The eccentric doctor arrived in a pin stripe suit and tie. His round wire framed glasses were positioned halfway down his nose as he awkwardly followed Ellen toward the president's office. His body leaned appreciably to his right side from the heavy weight of the gigantic medical bag he toted. It was his constant companion.

"I got here as quickly as possible, Mr. President. Ellen said that you needed some relief," Abramson began in a distinct German accent. The doctor had lived in the United States for nearly thirty years, but his accent never left him. From a base in New York he built up a client list that included some of the most prominent people in the United States. Athletes, Hollywood celebrities, authors and even politicians called upon him. The addictive quality of his amphetamine cocktails guaranteed a good many return clients.

"Glad to see you're still doing house calls doc," the President said, gritting his teeth in pain. "Thanks for coming here on such short notice. I could sure use your help."

"Let me take a look," Abramson said as he pulled up a chair and set down his black leather bag. He took out a needle, syringe and two bottles of his medicine, and loosened the president's back brace.

"Where's the discomfort?" the doctor asked, as his wrinkled face scrutinized the President's back.

"The usual places," the President twisted his arm behind himself and pointed awkwardly at the locations on his back. Abramson sank the needle deep into the offending muscle. Kelly exhaled sharply.

Relief traveled up the president's back like rising water in a fountain. Whatever Sid Abramson used in his mysterious formulas, it was a miracle as far as the President was concerned.

"Thanks again, doctor."

"I'm going to leave you this." It was a medicine bottle, not nearly as effective as his injections but useful in a pinch. "And remember; call me right away if the pain returns. If it still feels as bad in a few hours, call me and I'll see you again right away. I am leaving town tomorrow afternoon, so don't hesitate."

Scott Kelly reappeared in the doorway as Dr. Abramson was getting ready to exit. He knew what time the doctor would be visiting.

"Good afternoon doctor," the Attorney General said, eyeing the man as if he were a criminal suspect.

"Good afternoon," Abramson nodded in acknowledgement as he departed. Scott Kelly remained in the doorway keeping his cold stare locked on Abramson until the little Sigmund Freud look-alike was out of sight.

He was certain the so-called doctor was up to something. His brother was too trusting; there was no talking to him about it. Regardless of his gut feelings, he had to concede that those shots helped the President. There was nothing he could do at the moment, but he was determined to find out what was in the mysterious vials.

Chapter 16

Hell's Angels

Grant Vadala was enjoying himself at a cocktail party held at the home of William Charles Lyon Garner, a wealthy man of British ancestry known for his graciousness and well-mannered charm. Garner was the owner of a large island which his family bought from the Montaukett Indians in 1639. The host was old fashion in his pretentions, and still liked to refer to himself as the 16th Lord of the Manor. He was married to a young woman, a former British model.

Grant stood in a semi-circle with friends. With a drink in one hand and an appetizer in the other, he faced the imposing front door. The smile on his face faded when his most hated rival, author Truitt Capp, arrived in the company of Jamie's sister, Leslie Radzinger, who he did not hold in much higher regard. Leslie wore a white mink coat, while Truitt sported a blue pin-striped suit with a bow tie. With his bubble-eyes protruding from his little round head, he reminded Grant of a fly.

Grant's friends noticed that his expression upon seeing Truitt was reminiscent of the way one might look if he had arrived home to an infestation of insects and reptiles. He looked ready to stomp on the little pest - not physically of course, but with words. Words were weapons for Grant, and he sharpened his tongue for moments like this. He considered Capp an annoying specimen of low moral and ethical standards; an irresponsible drinker, a drug user, and a facilitator of rumors, gossip, and trouble, seemingly wherever he went. Worse, he was a rival – both professionally and socially. It offended Grant to think he had to compete with such trash. *Perhaps that is why he and Leslie get along so well,* Grant thought sarcastically.

But in reality Truitt had a keen eye for details that others missed. His perceptive observations about the people around him were memorable, if not always welcome. If he and Grant could only have gotten along for more than 30 seconds, they might have been surprised to discover that they shared some valuable insights and opinions. Both were talented writers. But it had to be said that Truitt was far more difficult to like. His coarseness and his vices too often won the day.

Truitt socialized with both Leslie and Jamie, and preferred Leslie. Jamie was too unilateral: she used people with no sense of obligations. She was known to bounce people out of her life like little rubber balls as they lost their utility. He sympathized and related more with the underdog Leslie, because she was younger, smaller, and more fragile. Although his acquaintance with the sisters was still warm, he harbored the possibility of writing about the two women later, if they ever betrayed his friendship or if he became desperate financially. He was aware that gossip always sold and he had plenty of juicy stories tucked away under his hat if he ever needed them.

Grant, on the other hand, tried to view the people around him and the world from a loftier peak. If he ever wrote a memoir he would tell the truth about the people in his life as he saw them, but he was not looking to capitalize monetarily on gossip. He didn't need money. His fondness for gossip was purely on its own terms.

In some ways Grant despised Leslie more than he did Jamie. To him, both women were gold diggers. That much was undeniable, but he had to admit that at least Jamie had some semblance of intelligence. Leslie he regarded, perhaps unfairly, as being quite dim-witted and shallow. He did not feel like having an exchange with Truitt this evening, although he was always prepared.

"*Hellll-low,* Grant," Truitt said with his annoying lisp.

"Good evening Truitt, Leslie," Grant nodded at the motley twosome. When he first saw them he wondered when Truitt would decide to spoil what had been a halcyon evening. But then he figured if they insisted on hanging around he may as well poke some fun, if it were warranted and tasteful. Sure enough, Truitt started in on Grant.

"Grant, I read your latest book. Tell me, what's the name of your ghostwriter?" Truitt was grinning from ear to ear after delivering his prepared line. But as always, Grant was ready.

"Dear Truitt, who was it that read my last book to you? I must say, at least they're choosing some quality literature for your bedtime stories these days." With that remark, the entire circle of people nearby broke out in laughter. Even Truitt had to smile as he knew Grant outfoxed him. The exchange of wits might have continued, but just as the men were about to commence a second round of bantering a portly man with round spectacles and a gray suit shouted out and waved "Truitt, Truitt! Over here!"

"Touché, Grant. I have to admit you hoodwinked me," he said, trying to save face as he and Leslie turned in the direction of the heavy set man. Grant and his friends snickered as the little fly and his companion slowly buzzed away toward the fat man.

After the unexpected encounter, Grant began to wonder who else might show up at the party. Would they see Jamie Kelly?

"Well Michael, much to my chagrin the masochist made it, chaperoned by her little fly. I had a feeling. It was too pleasant of an evening, something had to go awry," he quipped with the dramatic tone of a movie narrator. Michael laughed at Grant's dry humor. "The only question now remaining is whether her sister, the sadist, will make an appearance."

On more than one occasion, Grant had explained to Michael the various psychological abnormalities of the Bene sisters. Growing up, they jealously battled for the affection of their playboy father. In the process, the fierce competition created what Grant characterized as an S&M relationship between the girls. Michael was having difficulty wrapping his mind around such a warped adolescent environment, with Jamie in the role of big sister torturing Leslie.

Worse yet, in the case of Jamie, Grant had described the relationship with her father as a semi-incestuous, leaving Michael's imagination to wander. He was told that Slick Bene, as he was nicknamed, at times behaved as if Jamie was his wife or a mistress causing some to question the nature of their relationship. According to Grant, Slick had even bragged to his daughter about his sexual conquests with the mothers of some of her college friends. Michael never had reason to doubt anything Grant said. Grant was not a liar and had an uncanny gift of discernment, but Michael was sometimes surprised by his friend's candor. In fact, Michael knew that Grant was speaking the truth because he was friends with a woman who knew Jamie during her college days. When he asked about Jamie, his friend assessed the relationship likewise, finding Slick's behavior strange and creepy.

"Are you saying the first lady is planning on coming?" he asked, trying to get his mind off the sick thoughts.

Sure enough, just as the words were uttered they could see her, arrayed in one of Vosco

Cassone's custom dresses, near the door, where she was being greeted by the host and hostess. Jamie caught Grant's eye and simply nodded as she made her way over to her sister and Truitt.

"She seems to be avoiding you," Michael observed.

"I'm afraid her mother and I had words at the White House a couple of years ago. Believe me the old crow had it coming."

"I'm sure she did."

"I hope that doesn't put me on Jamie's list."

"What list?" Michael asked, confounded.

"She keeps a list of people. A hit list of sorts, for revenge purposes," Grant explained. "She probably learned it from her mother. She once told me 'revenge is sweeter than love.'"

"Atrocious"

"They're a remarkable family indeed," Grant sneered.

* * *

Meanwhile on the other side of the room, Truitt and Princess Leslie were busy visiting some friends when Jamie came over.

"Hi Leslie, hello Truitt" Jamie said in her soft voice as the two sisters shared a brief hug.

"I'm glad you could make it," Leslie said with a smile.

"With your schedule we weren't sure you would," Truitt added.

"Thanks, I was able to sneak away."

He knew it was a charade whenever these two got together, but Truitt played along. The two sisters were engaging in small talk when Paul, Truitt's rotund friend with the round glasses waddled over. He asked if anyone had a camera because he wanted a picture with the first lady. Scrutinizing her as she posed with his friend Paul, Truitt once again sensed that here was a very phony woman. He thought of her as an artful impersonator. She was impersonating 'Mrs. Kelly'. Her behavior struck him as odd, beyond fake but almost scripted. A feeling that there was more to Jamie than was visible nagged at him. Perhaps unreal was the best adjective. She struck him as an actress, or a character he might create for one of his books.

Moments later, an attractive woman came over to join the conversation. Truitt curiously perceived that both Jamie and Leslie did not like other women. *Female misogynists,* he thought. It would be funny if only it wasn't true. As for men, they used them for their own benefit. They're like geisha girls, it dawned on him. Breaking his deep thought was the gentlemanly voice of their host, William Garner.

"Is everyone having a pleasant time?" he asked politely.

"Oh, yes, it's been delightful. You have a marvelous place," Leslie answered.

Garner turned to Jamie. "I'm especially happy you were able to attend, Mrs. Kelly."

"Oh, thank you Mr. Garner, it was so nice of you to invite me." Jamie replied. Truitt noticed she had a surreal tendency to stare deep into one's eyes, nodding her head endlessly with a mesmerizing trance-like state. It was bizarre, even creepy. She spoke so softly that people had to strain their ears to hear what she had to say.

"Let's move to the den area," Garner told the eight to ten guests gathered in the immediate area. "We'll have coffee and cognac." The guests followed Garner to the nearby room.

After a few minutes of visiting, Jamie drew a cigarette and was a little surprised that no hand offered a flame. A little irritated she picked up an opulent cigarette lighter which belonged to Garner's wife from the nearby coffee table. Made of gold and engraved, the cigarette lighter was extremely valuable. Jamie lit her cigarette and slipped the lighter into her purse. Across the room, Mr. Garner observed the sleight of hand and became perplexed about what course of action he should take.

Garner was convinced that she did not do it by mistake, since he noticed she examined it for a moment or two in admiration. Thinking quickly, he grabbed a cigar out of his humidor and pretended that he did not know where to find his wife's lighter.

He began asking around if anyone had seen it and when Jamie did not answer he asked her directly by saying, "Mrs. Kelly, have you seen my wife's cigarette lighter? I believe you used it last."

Gazing into his eyes trance-like, Jamie replied softly, "I have no idea."

She eventually left the gathering with the lighter still her in purse. Garner was bewildered and paralyzed by such reprehensible behavior. He was astonished that the woman the press so admired would do such a thing. Overcome with shock and not wanting to make a scene, he could not decide how to handle such unethical behavior. He thought, *this is unpardonable, but what can I do? Call the police and have her arrested? Or throw her against a wall and frisk her?* In such an awkward position, he decided to do nothing. He acquiesced.

Chapter 17

Enter Lew Ohlman

It was September 1, 1963. Inside the Roosevelt hotel in downtown New Orleans, intelligence operative Lew Ohlman lay on a king-sized bed beside his young mistress, Julie Cary Parker. She was only nineteen years old, but a brilliant young scientist, a prodigy who had accomplished feats in her high school laboratory in rural Florida that only a few universities in the nation had achieved. As a contract employee of the FBI and CIA, one of his New Orleans assignments was to watch over the young cancer researcher. Parker was so unusually gifted that she was selected for early entry into medical school in exchange for her work as an intern in laboratories conducting cancer studies. She was fast-tracked into Tulane medical school on the recommendation of the school's former chief of surgery, Dr. Oxner. Oxner had also been president of the American Cancer Society and founder of a large medical center just outside the city. Oxner was one of the first doctors to link cigarette smoking to lung cancer. He was also a virulent anti-communist.

Ohlman was assigned to keep on eye on the young researcher, but in fact, he couldn't keep his eyes off her. He knew it was against protocol, but the two became lovers. They

weren't far apart in age, but still he seemed
world-weary next to the studious girl lying
beside him. He introduced her to the cloak and
dagger universe of espionage and his unique
experience of growing up in New Orleans and
later living behind the iron curtain of Russia.
Along the way he had inadvertently shared
sensitive information and introduced her to
people she wasn't supposed to know. They worked
together at a coffee company, front jobs setup
for them to hide their real work. Complicating
matters further, both were married; from the
first time their eyes met, they were tangled in
secrets.

He stared at the hotel ceiling, lost in
thought. He was aware of his infidelity, aware
that his job was in jeopardy, but he worried
about bigger things.

"Tomorrow I have to go back to Florida,"
Julie sighed. She dreaded the long drive with
her controlling husband. Just the thought made
her sick. Over the summer, she had fallen in
love with Lew. Her husband was away for weeks
at a time working on drilling rigs in the Gulf
of Mexico. She was young and didn't take to
living alone. Lew had been sent to protect her,
and she wanted him to rescue her from her life.
She was only nineteen, but already felt trapped
by men who capitalized on her idealism.

"All I wanted to do when I came here was to
save people from cancer," she sobbed. Her dream
of curing the disease was over, and the rest of
her dreams seemed to be dying along with it.

Lew held her in his arms until she caught her breath.

They had plans to run away to Mexico, but neither of them knew when that would be. She couldn't imagine what it would feel like to miss him. Julie studied him, trying to capture his face in her memory.

His pale blue-gray eyes seemed to take in everything while looking at nothing; he was smarter than he appeared, and that made him a good employee. He blended in. He wasn't small, but he was lean and rangy and somewhat drab. You could look right through him, if you weren't paying attention. If you were paying attention, and the light was right, he was halfway handsome. Sandy hair was receding early from a high, intelligent forehead. He had fine bones: high cheekbones, a strong chin, and a sort of permanent smirk on his little mouth. Depending on the set of his cryptic smile he could look perfectly amiable or acidly mocking.

What Julie saw was a good man in an untenable position. He was a patriot: a former marine, a man who had risked his life as an espionage agent. He entered the Soviet Union in the guise of a defector, and made it back alive. Now there was talk that he might be ordered to infiltrate another communist country: Cuba. The plan was for him to smuggle a cancer-causing bioweapon, which Julie had helped create, into the island country. He would hand it over to another operative, who would administer the poison to Fidel Castro. He

hoped that would be the end of the grisly
mission – but he doubted it.

He turned and took her into his arms. "I
shouldn't have gotten you involved in all these
things," he said. "I didn't realize it would
turn out this way. You know too much, and so do
I. We've shared too much information. It's
become dangerous."

"It isn't your fault," she replied.

She was right to a point. The secret lab
used to create the cancer causing injections
wasn't his idea, but it was a reason why Dr.
Oxner, the head of the project, had brought
Julie to New Orleans in the first place. Oxner
had two labs running simultaneously, one was a
legitimate university laboratory used to study
cancer and hopefully find a cure. The other was
top secret and its purpose was to create a
cancer causing weapon. Ohlman inadvertently
brought Julie into the second project by
introducing her to Dan Farris, mistakenly
thinking she was to be working with Farris.
Once Oxner came back to town it was too late to
undo the mix up and he decided to have her work
in both labs.

How strange fate had been, she mused. Since
high school, her main goal was to save peoples'
lives by finding a cure for cancer, the disease
that killed her beloved grandmother. In order
to cure cancer she concluded she had to study
the cells to see what made them grow, which she
did using fish and mice as a high school
student – a feat that only a few university
laboratories could replicate. One of the

brightest high school scientists in the state of Florida, she was given a scholarship to Tulane. She thought she would be trained to cure the disease, not create biological weapons to kill people.

After she expressed her outrage about testing the cancer-causing bioweapon on healthy prisoners, Dr. Oxner pulled her scholarship and kicked her out of the internship and medical school. He would make arrangements for her to obtain a job in Florida, but he was finished with her. Oxner and others viewed using the unsuspecting "volunteers" as a necessary evil. They had to discover if the weapon would work before they sent it to Cuba.

"Dr. Oxner was so angry he told me I was lucky he didn't knock my teeth out for writing that note," she repeated to Lew. "He said that if I open my mouth and something happens to me, he's not responsible."

"In hindsight, you probably should have told him how you felt verbally, but I agree with what you wrote." he sighed as picked up his *Pocket Aristotle* book off the nightstand. Lew loved to read and recently they had been discussing Aristotle's view on philosophy and ethics. "Like Dan told you they don't want a paper trail."

"I'm not a murderer! This violates the Hippocratic Oath and every other ethical law. Why didn't Oxner tell me they planned to use it experimentally on unsuspecting humans?" she asked, still venting. She went along with the weapons project when the participants appealed to her patriotism and explained that its purpose was to assassinate the evil communist leader Fidel Castro. By participating she might help prevent a World War III. After the missile crisis that explanation seemed plausible. Wasn't it better to sacrifice one man than the entire planet?

Another convoluted justification Julie was given by others involved in the project was that if Castro was killed it might actually save President Kelly's life, because it would fragment the growing coalition of his opponents. It was no secret that there was dangerous opposition to him, especially among anti-communists and southerners.

They convinced her, initially. But the possibility of numerous individuals being murdered like lab animals to assure efficacy of the weapon never dawned on her. She became emotional when she realized she would have a hand in so many needless deaths. It was more than she could handle.

"I told you too much about operations you shouldn't know. I was so happy to have someone to talk with I didn't think about the consequences. Information like what takes place in Manister's office."

Manister was one of Lew's superiors. A retired FBI man from Chicago, he ran a small PI office in town. To the outside world, Manister's office, if they noticed it all, appeared to be exactly that - a small PI firm. Julie learned from Lew that it was actually a secret headquarters through which the FBI, CIA,

Office of Naval Intelligence, and other covert organizations conducted business. Anti-Castro Cuban rebels were armed through the office as well as the infiltration of leftist groups.

"I also know too much," he continued, "about the bioweapon."

"But you should, since you're going to be carrying it. Aren't you taking it to Cuba?" she asked.

"The way they're acting lately I don't know." He looked hard at her, and then turned his attention back to that spot on the ceiling. "I actually think they plan on killing me."

"What? Why?" she asked fearfully.

"It's because I know too much."

"You mean about the project?" she asked.

"Yes, but not just that," Lew said, seeing the worry on her face. "You didn't do anything wrong. I was supposed to spy on the lab for the Company, to make sure it went as planned. And watch over you."

"What do you mean about 'the way they're acting'?"

"I've noticed that my superiors are keeping a lot of information from me – more than usual. They don't trust me. Also, they're holding me back in the organization. I haven't been promoted. None of these are good signs. They act as though I'm expendable."

Chapter 18

The Doctor

Doctor Alden Oxner was revered in the medical world. He was a man who never slept. He would perform surgeries, attend conferences, meet with patients and businessmen and get much of his sleep on airplanes in between business trips. As one of the world's top surgeons he was in a position to meet interesting and influential people and to move in those circles of society.

Over the years he befriended businessmen, many of whom had suffered monetarily as a result of the communist revolution in Cuba. Oxner sympathized deeply and helped to form an organization to stop the spread of communism in the Americas.

Clearly, if the domino effect was to be halted in the Americas, Castro needed to be eliminated. Killing him was a top priority, but how? Working alongside the CIA, Oxner's anti-communist organization established a secret lab in New Orleans where a biological weapon could be created to assassinate their enemies. To that end, Oxner covertly built a small team of specialists.

Shortly after the incident with Julie, Oxner held a meeting with a few of the project's backers to discuss its progress.

Oxner could work a room like a politician when required. Also like a politician, he could be charming in a group, but his temper was a force to be reckoned with.

In attendance was a representative for Charles Merchant, one the richest men in Texas. Merchant and Oxner were close friends. Over the years he had helped Oxner with a few projects, including this one. Merchant actually gave the doctor a Cadillac each year, and helped him acquire land when Oxner was building his clinic. Now it was Oxner's turn to pony up. Getting rid of Castro would certainly be greatly appreciated and a way of returning all his friend's favors.

The CIA was also present at the meeting, represented by Bob Angler. As the head of counterintelligence, Angler was actually number two or three in the CIA hierarchy, depending on who you asked. He was organized crime's most loyal man in the CIA and received his orders from the power elite of international organized crime. Such men were above the Italian regional lieutenants who were used as mere errand boys and who received all the unwanted headlines in the press.

The current CIA director was new and often kept out of the loop, making Angler far more powerful than he appeared on paper. He too was concerned about President Kelly completely disbanding the CIA and placing it under the FBI. Kelly had already made the opening moves, having fired the top two men in the CIA - Angler's friends. He considered himself lucky to still be around, but he feared he might not be much longer if Kelly was reelected.

To Angler and his friends in the agency, Oxner's secret lab was only a side bet. They had other projects throughout the country. In fact, in New Orleans alone they had other doctors, brain specialists, working on electrode implants in the skull designed to control human thoughts and actions. For some assignments, the latter project was further developed and had more utility and potential. Doctors were able to partition a person's brain so that he or she had two separate personalities and limited memory when not in that personality. Thus, they were able to create an unwitting spy or assassin without the subject himself even knowing. Just the year before, in 1962, a movie came out about mind controlled assassins called *The Manchurian Candidate*. From his experience, Angler knew the film was in many ways an accurate depiction of what the CIA had been able to accomplish.

The men settled in and Doctor Oxner began to discuss the bioweapon project. He carefully avoided mentioning Julie Parker's dismissal, knowing that even the perception that any information concerning the secret lab had leaked out would be dangerous. Instead, he focused on the success of the device.

"We've finally achieved our aim," Oxner proudly announced to the small group. "The formula accomplishes our goal in three to four weeks," he continued. He could see Angler smile slightly, like a macabre Mona Lisa. "We've tested it on prisoners," he continued as he described the result in greater detail. The formula caused death by "natural causes" in less than a month. The men looked at each other. They now had the power to murder their enemies without suspicion. And each man and the faction he represented had different ideas about who was to be considered an enemy. This time, they all agreed Castro was an antagonist, but each man was silently creating his own list of who would be next.

"I'm happy to hear the good news. Has the project remained discreet?" Angler probed.

"Yes, to my satisfaction it has," Oxner replied. "There's been no paper trail," he added. He wasn't going to mention sending Julie Parker off to Florida because of her note. Just thinking about her note got his blood boiling. That was a can of worms he preferred not to open. He wasn't going to say something that could land him in the trunk of a car.

"And Dr. Sheridan?" Angler continued to probe.

"Nothing to worry about there. She's very unassuming, a widow. She keeps a very private life," Oxner reassured. He knew the CIA was keeping a close eye on the people in the project. Angler didn't ask about Lew Ohlman or his pilot friend Dan Farris. They were both linked to the agency, so there wasn't much Oxner could tell Angler that he didn't already know.

Thankfully Angler didn't ask about Julie Parker. Had he done so, Oxner had a prepared answer: he would tell Angler not to worry, that she was a book smart kid but wasn't a problem, and that she had gotten married and decided to move back to Florida. He was furious just thinking about her. She wrote her message to him on paper and left it with his secretary, who read it aloud to him over the phone! There was to be no paper trail! Teenager or not, stupid mistakes could get people killed.

Oxner decided to go on the offensive and ask a question of his own. The Company had trained Lew Ohlman on how to handle, transport and administer the weapon, but Oxner had concerns. He learned that Ohlman had gotten close with Julie Parker and he wondered what he was thinking. The young man rarely talked. As far as he was concerned, Julie Parker was out of the picture and Ohlman was expendable.

"How will you use Ohlman?" Oxner probed.

"I'm not sure yet," Angler answered.

Oxner could tell the way he said it that he was holding something back. They never gave anyone the entire picture. *All these guys are the same,* he thought.

"We'll probably send him to Mexico and let someone else bring the device to the island. We have another assignment setting up in Texas for Ohlman. We will need him there. We'll move his family to Dallas. But for now he can wait in Louisiana for our call," Angler explained with a tone of finality.

"I see." Oxner did not want to become too inquisitive with Angler. His friend Merchant could probably fill him in to what was happening in Texas.

Chapter 19

Have Bioweapon, Will Travel

For the first three weeks of September Lew Ohlman stayed at home in New Orleans always near the phone. Arrangements were made by the CIA to have his pregnant wife and daughter relocated to a friend's home in Irving, Texas. Delivering the bioweapon was an assignment he needed to complete before he could join them. That is of course if he survived.

Over the past few months he had come to no longer trust his superiors. Their strange behavior and disrespect set off warning alarms. He wasn't sure exactly what they had planned for him but he couldn't help from thinking the worst. One of his higher level handlers had used three different last names, all beginning with the letter B.

What does this man think of me that he can't remember which fictitious surname he used last? Ohlman thought.

To him it was a sign of dishonesty, disrespect and an insult to his intelligence. More disturbing yet was that he saw clues that his superiors considered him to be expendable. He knew too much and as a "returned defector" he might never be fully trusted. He feared that the agency might set him up in some way, especially after Manister had him pose as a pro-communist on the streets of New Orleans, where he handed out leaflets supporting communist Cuba. It was even arranged for him to be a guest on a radio show and debate on behalf of Marxism. The purpose of these assignments, Manister told him, was to make it easier for him to infiltrate leftist groups around New Orleans and that it would help him later when he was sent into Cuba.

Thoughts of fleeing the country and meeting up with Julie Parker entered his mind. He dreamt of it. They had even planned it. However, reality reminded him that he was inside a machine he could not exit. He was in a bad position, *there were no good moves left on the chessboard,* he mused. He had obligations, to his country, his family, and to President Kelly, whose life he was convinced was in danger. He was a man bound by duty. He couldn't abandon everything, at least not yet. Despite his premonitions he had to play it straight.

Finally at the end of September he received an early morning call, "It's time to travel, are you all packed?" It was Gus Manister's vile voice. Lew understood what he meant. The prisoner had died. The bioweapon worked and it was time for him to make the delivery to Cuba via Mexico.

"Yeah, I'm all set. I just have one quick errand to run." He had two suitcases waiting, already packed. He just had to pick up his unemployment check, cash it, and he'd be ready.

"We'll meet at 9 like we planned," Manister said in his always serious voice.

Assassination Point Blank

"Yes, sir," Ohlman was told there would be a meeting the day he received the call to review the plan and then he would leave for Mexico the next morning.

"Tomorrow Hale will take you for part of the trip. We'll tell you more when we meet." Hale White was a pilot, and a Manister partner. Lew wished his friend Dan Farris could fly him instead. Dan was eccentric but very intelligent and more trustworthy than these other men. And having known Ohlman for years he shared more information and treated him with greater respect, which made Lew feel more comfortable. *But wishing was for widows and orphans*, Lew thought. He was stuck with Hale.

The next morning Lew Ohlman, Gus Manister, Hale White along with a man from Texas who was known to be a carrier for Lionel Jones met for breakfast. The plan was already formulated but before they could leave Manister said that they first had to wait for Chester Showen, an important New Orleans businessman.

Showen was yet another of Ohlman's CIA superiors. Like Manister, he was gray-haired and middle-aged. He was a businessman about ten years younger than Gus but with a better personality, which wasn't saying much considering Manister's repulsive demeanor. Showen was tall, thin, and more sophisticated than Manister, but still he was a swinging cat, the New Orleans vernacular for a homosexual. That didn't bother Lew though, having lived in New Orleans there weren't many things he hadn't seen.

Assassination Point Blank

Showen was a CIA operative and the director of the International Trade Mart. Having those two positions, naturally Ohlman figured that the financing and logistics of many secret espionage projects were done through Showen. Ohlman was unaware that Showen also served on the board of a shadowy corporation that had ties to international organized crime, money laundering banks in Switzerland, and the national intelligence agencies of foreign countries. What he did know was that Showen was instrumental in assisting Dr. Oxner on the cancer project and at times was even a hands-on participant. He even drove members of the secret lab, including Ohlman, to a mental hospital in a remote location in Louisiana to begin testing the cancer causing injections on humans.

Once he arrived, Showen didn't waste any time and got right down to business.

"These go with you to Austin," he said with a stern look as he handed the Texan a stack of files and an envelope. Based on the names mentioned Ohlman concluded that the paperwork was headed for Lionel Jones' lawyer.

He then turned to Lew, "And this is for you," he said as he handed him a zipper bag partially opening it to show its contents. It was cleverly disguised to look like a lunch pouch with potato chips and a piece of fruit inside. The deadly contents were stored in a thermos-like container which preserved the cancer cells.

"When you get to Houston you'll switch this one out for a refreshed batch," Showen instructed avoiding eye contact. He explained that another batch had been flown ahead and stored in a lab.

I wonder why I'm bringing this one, if they have cancer cells with a longer shelf life already in safe storage in Houston, Ohlman thought. It didn't make sense. He knew Showen was being shifty. He wondered if Dr. Oxner knew about the material flown ahead. It was hard to say where Dr. Oxner's oversight ended and where it drifted off into the CIA's black hole or if Oxner himself was a part of a greater conspiracy. As respectable as he was, even Dr. Oxner was a wild card. Nobody knew for sure what he truly believed. What Ohlman did know was that none of these men were fond of President Kelly, despite the fact that the man was the world's best chance for peace. And now, having heard that bioweapon material was sent ahead made him suspicious. *And what about this one he's giving me? What is its purpose? If I'm to drop it off in Houston it certainly isn't going to Mexico or Cuba. Once in Houston where will it go? What would happen to it?* He mused.

After receiving the material and instructions from Showen, the group split to go their own ways. The Texan would be flying straight to Austin on a separate plane, departing out of a different airport. Ohlman would travel with Hale White. Gus Manister and Chester Showen would stay in Louisiana.

When Ohlman and White arrived at the airport they found a Hispanic man waiting for them in the double engine aircraft. It was a plane often used in the energy industry for oil field personnel. They would fly in a triangular pattern at top speed over the state of Texas to three different cities; Austin, Dallas and finally Houston where Lew would catch a bus for Laredo and cross the border into Mexico, Hale explained.

During the flight, small talk was at a minimum and it quickly died to silence. "There's a sleeping bag in back if you want to get some rest," Hale said loudly from the pilot seat as the plane's engines rumbled in the background. "We're going to Austin and Dallas first because there's some business to take care of before we drop you off in Houston." The Hispanic man, Jorge remained silent in the co-pilot seat next to him.

Ohlman found a blue sleeping bag in a storage compartment and tried to get some rest. Thoughts of the odd travel schedule between cities, the Texan flying to Austin with paperwork and envelopes for Lionel Jones, and the behavior of those around him heightened his suspicion. Why were they keeping him in the dark?

He thought back about conversations in New Orleans he overheard when he was around anti-Castro people (prior to him posing as pro-Cuba). There were discussions about assassinating Fidel Castro and sometimes how those same people wished someone would kill

President Kelly. Now seeing two airplanes flying questionable material to Austin he believed that whatever the plotters were scheming pointed to the Texas capital. Ohlman was convinced that all the intrigue and secrecy went beyond just attempting to assassinate Castro. He suspected President Kelly was also being targeted for assassination. Were they setting him, Lew Ohlman, up as a scapegoat? He sure had that feeling. But if the method to kill the president was with a cancer causing weapon, why would they need him to be a patsy? In that case the man's death would simply appear to be a terrible misfortune, just like Castro. There was something missing to this puzzle.

As he gave it more thought, his hypothesis that both leaders were targets made sense. All of his speculation did, except the nagging feeling that he was being betrayed. That he couldn't quite explain. What was indisputable was that President Kelly was unpopular with many factions including elements in the CIA. And now the agency had its hands on the weapon project, which they planned to use to eliminate their enemy in Cuba. Why not eliminate two enemies? It was possible. Who could know what these men were thinking.

If the cabal's base extended into Austin, he wanted to leave a clue, witnesses, a paper trail, some type of evidence to prove he was there. That way, if he was indeed being setup as a fall guy he would have witnesses, in addition to his testimony, to prove where he was at a particular time. By doing so, even if he died there would still be evidence linking him to the lab project, the plotters, and his whereabouts. *If they are setting me up, they certainly would not want to admit that I work for the CIA and that I was being flown around today by Manister's CIA operative partner and that I was in Austin and Dallas when I'm supposed to be on a bus in Houston,* he thought. His head throbbed as the plane bounced up and down on some turbulence. On the flight, instead of sleeping he managed to contrive a way to prove he was in Austin.

"Get your seatbelt on, we're getting ready to land," Hale yelled over his shoulder as the front end of the plane tipped noticeably downward.

A few minutes later they finally landed in Austin where there was a car nearby waiting for them.

"Jorge can drop you off to get yourself some lunch and get paid before he takes me where I need to go to deliver this package." Hale said.

"I know a lunch place that's not too far away," Lew replied thinking quickly. "It's near the Selective Service office, over by the governor's offices. Can you drop me off over there?" He was already thinking of a creative way to try to lay down a paper trail. Jorge looked at Hale. He nodded that it was ok.

"That's a good location," Hale agreed. "We'll make a call to have you get your envelope over there," he said referring to the payment for Ohlman's mission to Mexico. It made Ohlman think. If the location was convenient that made it more likely that the orchestrators of the mission were in the area of the governor's office.

A short car ride later he was dropped off at the lunchroom. He ate a quick meal then hustled on foot to pay a visit to the nearby the Selective Services office, ostensibly to discuss his Marine discharge, and thereby creating an Austin witness in the process.

"Why hasn't this been changed?" he exclaimed loudly to the woman behind the counter, causing a commotion as he complained about the status. The status hadn't been changed and had been reviewed by Peter "Red" Farleigh, Under Secretary of the Navy. Lew had a lawyer, Drew Anderson, in New Orleans working on the matter and had written letters to the Secretary of the Navy, Frank Korsey. To make a fuss over it now in Austin didn't make much sense, but he was interested in creating a paper trail. While in the office he raised his voice, to make sure he would be remembered. After a few minutes of ruckus behavior, enough to raise a scene but not enough that they would call security, he was satisfied that he would now be remembered. He then left the building to return to the lunchroom where Jorge and Hale would pick him up. A man met him there with an envelope, payment for his taking the cancer material into Mexico. Ohlman was picked up a short time later and brought back to the airport.

"We're flying to Dallas and then we'll take you to Houston," Hale White said as he wasted no time preparing the plane for takeoff. It was a short flight. "You'll have time to run some errands," he said knowing Ohlman was concerned about his wife and daughter and wanted to make contingent living arrangements for her in case they needed to move.

"Thank you. If I have time I also need to see a friend." His friend Jake Rubin, a nightclub owner and another silent financier of the secret laboratory, wanted to see him. Lew had known Jake Rubin since he was boy. Decades earlier, Jake had moved to Dallas from Chicago. Jake's nightclub business in Dallas engaged in book making and other illegal activity. It ultimately fell under the territory of the organized crime boss in New Orleans. Both Jake Rubin and Lew's uncle worked under the crime boss. As a result, from time to time Rubin came to New Orleans on business.

Jake Rubin, like practically all the men in Ohlman's life was another enigma. Before the revolution, he was involved in the casino business in Cuba and later in running guns to the island to arm the rebels for the CIA. So, even though Jake was in organized crime he also worked for the CIA. There were plenty of people who worked on a contract basis. Lew understood it well. He was in a similar situation. He worked for Naval Intelligence but was loaned out to the FBI and assisted the CIA. Such was the labyrinthine world of espionage and the underworld. Lew was fond of Jake. He almost considered him a relative.

***

"Hi there Lew," Jake said with a friendly smile as soon as he spotted him in the club. Built like a spark plug, Jake was in his early fifties but he was in the physical shape of a man twenty years younger. He came over and gave Lew a firm hand shake. "You're making your trip today. There's something I'd like you to pick up for me while you're down there."

"What's that?" Lew wondered what it would be as he already had a lot on his mind.

"Some laetrile, you know the anti-cancer drug. It's illegal here in the states but it's legal in Mexico. Can you look around while you're down there and see if you can find some?" Rubin peeled a few large bills from his wallet. Rubin was a financier of the lab and may have been concerned about the cancer being contagious Lew thought. Or, more likely, Rubin knew someone with cancer who wanted the laetrile. His patrons were heavy drinkers and smokers so that was possible too. Lew didn't ask any questions.

"Sure Jake, you know you can always count on me." He did similar favors for his uncle who was a bookmaker in New Orleans so this request was no big deal if he could find what Jake was seeking. Lew's uncle had once offered him work in the business, but he turned it down. He wanted to serve his country. Besides, in some cases, to really advance up the ladder in the underworld you might have to kill someone at some point, he realized. These were the type of guys who could be laughing and opening Christmas gifts with their long time buddy one minute then murdering him and stuffing his body in a car trunk the next, if such actions were required. To be in Jake's business there were times you had to be that cold.

Lew wasn't cut from the same cloth as Jake. *It was bad enough if I had to shoot someone in the line of duty as a Marine*, he thought. While in the Marines he was discharged and moved into Naval Intelligence. Then the Office of Naval Intelligence decided to loan him out to the CIA for certain assignments. The deeper involved he became in espionage, the more it reminded him of organized crime. The two crossed paths so many times it was hard to differentiate between them.

Before he left the club he telephoned Sadie Oroyo, a Spanish speaking intelligence operative in Dallas that he hoped might have contacts down in Mexico City. He also got word that his superiors would make living arrangements for his wife. As he left the club to meet with Oroyo he wondered what Jake Rubin's actual role was in all this intrigue. It seemed that everybody around him was involved but nobody knew the whole picture. The same was true for both the anti-Castro mission as well as the dangers posed to President Kelly. After a brief meeting with Oroyo in which she gave him the address of a place to stay in Mexico City, he was back on the plane finally heading for Houston.

***

"Good luck on your trip," Hale said as the men stood on the tarmac in Houston. A car was already there idling, ready to take Ohlman to pickup the refreshed cancer material and then bring him to the Bus station.

"Bye, Hale," Ohlman replied, already exhausted from spending the day of flying around the state of Texas. He quickly exchanged the zipper bag for the refreshed version and caught a bus to begin his journey into Mexico. The scientist in Houston told him the new batch would last two days longer. But he was still perplexed why he was given the first bag if they already had flown one ahead with a longer life span waiting in Houston. It made him suspicious that perhaps they were playing the old switcheroo. Perhaps he dropped off the real formula and picked up a fake? But if that was the case; why?

Once the bus had traveled about an hour outside of Houston he noticed how bare the Texas landscape appeared. The route traveled through mostly remote countryside on its way to Laredo. His view out the window wasn't good but in the darkness he could still make out the flat dry sandy prairie land with an occasional tree or tumbleweed near the road. Normally he would have been bored, if it were not for the deadly bioweapon stored under his seat. He brought a paperback book for the journey but he continued to reread the same sentence, so he spent most of the time thinking. He was anxious, but not about smuggling the weapon into Mexico, although that was no small matter. It wasn't the first time he had undertaken a risky operation. He had participated in life threatening missions as a Marine, as a spy in Russia, and even while running errands for organized crime as favors for his uncle, who was a bookmaker in New Orleans. But none of his previous experiences were filled with as much cloak and dagger secrecy as this.

The journey was over 1,000 miles; more than two thirds of it was on the other side of the border. After the first long bus ride he finally made it across into Mexico without incident. A border guard merely looked at the bag, thought it was his lunch and waved him on through.

The second leg of trip was longer and less comfortable, but at least he was relieved of one worry, having already crossed the border successfully. Over the road noise and rattling sounds he could hear only Spanish spoken on the new bus he caught in Nuevo Laredo in route to Mexico City. Most of the talk was too fast for him to comprehend. That was fine. He wasn't much for talking anyway. His attention was now focused on the men he worked for in the CIA and their mysterious plans. After seven hundred miles of bouncing, rocking, and squeaking down the Mexican highway he arrived at his destination in Mexico City.

Chapter 20

Confidant and Coworker

Although it had only been six weeks since her C-section, Jamie Kelly handled her horse effortlessly through the autumn Virginia landscape as she rode beside her long time friend and confidant Clyde Lighthouse. Oppressive melancholy still hung heavily upon her after the death of her 3 day old son. She hoped a horseback ride through the countryside would get her mind off the tragedy. Her body still ached from the surgery and her psyche was even more damaged from what she perceived as unfair treatment she received from the Kelly family. When Jamie became despondent she believed that everyone in the family was an adversary working against her. The men in the family viewed her as property; like a piece of furniture or real estate. And the women treated her like an outsider and never understood her point of view or sympathized with her misfortunes.

Her riding partner Clyde was a tall man, whose easy elegance and quiet dignity could easily fit in with majestic British nobility. Like Jamie he enjoyed horseback riding, fox hunting, foreign cultures and travel. He was born in Europe and had traveled widely, both as a youth and as an officer in US naval intelligence.

Assassination Point Blank

An east coast blue blood, Clyde's great-grandfather was a railroad baron. Academically he followed in his father's footsteps and attended Yale University where his enrollment was interrupted by World War II. Upon his return from the service, he was tapped for membership in the Order of Skull and Bones, as was his father. Politics, espionage, banking, and the media were favored professions for men in the Secret Brotherhood. It was natural that after graduation Clyde was hired by the CIA.

Jamie Kelly had many friends and acquaintances like Clyde. In fact, a good number of her friends were men, many of whom had ties to Yale University, secret societies, and the intelligence community.

As Clyde and Jamie maneuvered their horses down the lower trail leading through the bottomland they could see in the distance the beautiful lush green Virginia countryside. They took in the fresh air and scenery. Cows could be heard mooing in a nearby pasture. The multicolored tree tops swayed slightly with the light breeze. The rolling hills and the greenery of the forest in the distance made it a beautiful place to ride. As they came to a clearing they slowed their horses.

Despite the peaceful surroundings, Jamie couldn't get her mind off her unhappy marriage. "You know Clyde, I don't feel appreciated around that family like I should," she complained bitterly.

"I know, Jamie," Clyde consoled. Clyde Lighthouse understood. He was no fan of the

Kelly's either. The family had thrown a monkey wrench into The Order's international money-making plans.

"I don't think you can fully understand Clyde. You're a man. Think about what I have to deal with. There are James' Hollywood girlfriends, and my sister-in-laws. I'm getting so tired of those toothy Mick girls. They are so unsophisticated and really annoying," Jamie grumbled with an air of arrogant disdain. Clyde found this last comment especially intriguing considering her family's own mysterious genealogy. Her grandfather on her paternal side had gone to great lengths to create an ancestry supposedly originating from an aristocratic French lineage. In reality, a little due diligence revealed that his claims were at best a fallacious embellishment, at worst an elaborate and total fabrication. But his efforts did serve the purpose of gaining family members entrance into several prestigious clubs and secret societies.

On her mother's side, it was claimed that the family's origin was from Ireland, which made Jamie's Irish ethnic slur more curious. Then there was her stepbrother, Grant Vadala, who had heard from his own mother that Jamie's maternal lineage was Jewish. Her mother's family for some time claimed to be related to a famous Civil War general, until the general's ancestors objected and Jamie's family relented. But none of this surprised Clyde; he had worked in the intelligence community on the east coast long enough to know that just about everything in this world was smoke and mirrors. There wasn't much he hadn't seen.

In her soft monotone voice Jamie continued to describe her dilemma. "People say that my sister-in-laws are such team players, but that is probably because they can't think for themselves."

"They're certainly not refined culturally like you," he agreed.

"I just lost my baby, Clyde, and the whole clan goes right back to business as if nothing happened," she cried. "What's wrong with these people? I feel like the world is moving ahead without me."

"I'm sorry about your loss and I know it's difficult. It's a shame to hear that they're treating you like that," Clyde answered carefully. Jamie was unstable anyway, but the trauma caused from losing the child had clearly made her fragile mental state worse.

"And James is such a tightwad," she complained. "I'm really getting sick of him having my secretary keep tabs on my spending. It's been going on for a long time, but now he's getting even worse. He is micromanaging my life. I can't even buy clothes any more without being under scrutiny. Doesn't he have better things to do as President of the United States?" she asked looking over as their horses slowly trotted side by side.

"It sounds like he can be quite controlling," Clyde replied sympathetically, while pulling the reigns back slightly to keep his horse traveling at an even trot.

"Controlling is putting it nicely, Clyde. My God, he's watching my every move, reading my mail. He even has Madeline working with Dante Parelli, a forensic accountant, counting every nickel I spend. For heaven's sake, my marriage is like a business transaction," she lamented, looking at Clyde with watery eyes.

"That's horrible Jamie, I'm sorry. He seems like such an easy going man. Who would think? I guess behind closed doors people act different."

"He *is* different behind closed doors. Have you ever seen him? He has a funny-looking body - with skinny toothpick legs that are out of proportion to the rest him," she remarked, cutting her husband down.

Clyde grinned.

"It's no laughing matter. Other women don't have to deal with this kind of nonsense, Clyde. Take a look at my sister. She's married and yet she is able to have men in her life who can give her anything she desires. It's not fair!" Her frustration was building into a vindictive rage.

He was aware that Jamie coveted her sister's rich friend Arion Ostratos. Rumor was that the feeling was mutual. Clyde understood the situation completely. Jamie was wildly jealous of her sister - or any woman who had what she wanted, for that matter. Ostratos was single, insanely rich, and inclined to spend his wealth freely on his mistresses.

Clyde laughed to himself as he visualized Ostratos' short toady appearance. It was especially funny after hearing Jamie criticize her husband's looks. She could not possibly find Arion Ostratos attractive, could she? This was about the mighty dollar. But he couldn't blame the two dames. Everyone was motivated by money, right? And Ostratos had plenty of it. He wondered if insecurities brought about from a dysfunctional childhood caused both sisters to put such a high importance on materialism. After ten years of marriage to James Kelly, Jamie appeared frustrated that she did not have the kind of discretion with the family's money that she hoped to gain. She had a point; if they were going to monitor and bridle her spending, what benefit was it if the family was one of the wealthiest in the United States?

"It's good for you to get this off your chest but remember you have to be patient. It'll work out."

"Patient? It could be five years, Clyde," she countered as if that were an eternity. "You know I've been wanting out for years. That Happy Birthday Mr. President song by his Hollywood whore last year was the last straw." The blonde sex symbol had since died, in mysterious fashion, but Jamie still could not conceal her jealously. "I can't take it anymore! I don't want to wait five more years!" she said getting visibly agitated.

"That performance was in bad taste. But the woman is dead and your husband will not be in office much longer," Lighthouse remarked confidently, as if he knew something the rest of the world did not, "and once he's out of the White House you can begin anew."

"I wish I could divorce him sooner. I hate campaigning with him and if he wins next year's election it will be four more years," she grumbled.

"There are ways to make that happen sooner," he said as they rode briskly back toward the house.

The weather had turned visibly worse during their ride; the wind had picked up and the sky turned gray. Their outing was winding down as they could see the farm house in the distance. The sky became dark and there came a sudden clap of thunder. It was the beginning of a six-day rain.

Chapter 21

Rituals, Rehearsals & Incantations Sept '63

Due to the loss of their baby, James and
Jamie hadn't enjoyed a pleasant weekend
together in months, and James wanted to give it
a try before winter. The weather was perfect
for a weekend in Newport, and a few days with
Red Farleigh and his family seemed well worth
the effort. Jamie's stepfather's family estate
on the shore was where they had celebrated
their wedding ten years earlier.

It was September 21, 1963. The autumn
equinox: the time of year when daylight seems
to surrender to darkness. Already there was a
chill in the air. On that Sunday afternoon, the
two families went for a cruise aboard the
president's yacht. Agents Aaron Godson and
Georgie Blair followed close behind in a
speedboat. The children played while the adults
socialized over a few drinks. Upon return to
the dock, Don Kanard, a White House
photographer, positioned himself to take films
of the two families.

"James, you can go on ahead with our
guests," Jamie said. "I'll catch up with you in
a few minutes."

"Ok dear, we'll see you inside," the
President replied as he gathered a few personal
items from the boat and led the group up the
sandy beach toward the mansion. The first lady

remained outside with Kanard. She called over the agents that were on duty.

With six Secret Service agents nearby she requested that they play along with her in a little movie skit. The plot of the skit was that President Kelly had been shot!

"Mr. Hellerman, please come here." Jamie called out to one of her Secret Service agents.

"Yes Mrs. Kelly, what can I do for you?" Big Troy asked as he strolled closer. His square shaped head and big hands and feet were reminiscent of Frankenstein.

"Remember? We are going to make a little movie and we need your help. Could you please drive the car up the driveway, then jump out and run into the house?"

"Oh, yes of course. Do you want me to bring the car up now?" Hellerman asked.

"No, wait until Don is ready. He will direct the film." Kanard was making his way up the beach toward the house. He carried a video camera to record the little skit. The first lady was so excited. The agents shared her enthusiasm. "And Cliff, be ready with your gun," Jamie told her favorite agent with a thrill in her voice.

"OK, now I want you to drive the car up," Kanard indicated to the agents once he positioned his camera on the side of the driveway. "When you see that rock," he said to Hellerman as he pointed to large round stone off to the side, "I want you to begin the action."

Big Troy nodded and then turned to Jamie. "Wait until I give the signal, then everyone starts their part."

The large car barreled up the incline, its tires screeched on the asphalt as it came to a sudden stop on the driveway near the front door. Hellerman and Hillman quickly jumped out of the car, the door remained open. As requested, Hillman pulled out his snub nose revolver for a moment to give the film greater effect. The first lady loved it.

The agents ran around in their dark suits and sunglasses following Kanard's instructions for the skit, all to the delight of the first lady. She was so happy playing actress she skipped around gleefully like a school girl.

The men were pleased to see her in such a good mood. They knew she always wanted to be an actress and so they played along with her by performing their roles. It was a bizarre request indeed: the little film portrayed the murder of the president.

At the end of the skit agent Aaron Godson turned to Big Troy Hellerman and asked, "So who killed the president?"

"Nobody knows," Big Troy grinned as he was walking back to the car.

"Well she sure seemed to enjoy it," laughed Blair as Hillman nodded with a smile. But what was this film? A prank, or a rehearsal? Some people said the equinox was a time for putting plans into motion; certainly the stars were aligning for change.

"Only sixty-six more days," someone said matter-of-factly, in a low voice.

Chapter 22

Domestic Disputes

After their return to the White House from their weekend in Newport, Kelly noticed that Jamie's temperamental swings were steeper and more frequent. Before opening the door of the Queen's suite to check on his wife, he stood in the hallway for a second wondering which Jamie would be there to greet him. Even before they moved to the White House the couple had been keeping separate bedrooms. The Queen's bedroom was where the First Lady slept. He stayed in the Lincoln bedroom. Earlier in the day she felt ill and failed to join him at a lunch meeting with a foreign dignitary and his wife. She was known to play "hooky" at times, particularly if she was disinterested in the guest or event. Finally, he cautiously opened the door. As he entered the room, he recognized the temperamental expression on her face.

"Are you feeling better?" he asked, careful of his tone, fully aware she would use the sick card to excuse not attending events and then afterward she would become mercurial and belligerent. He spotted a magazine lying on the bed. On the cover was a blonde beauty wearing a shiny gray low cut sequin cocktail dress. Her large breasts and a sexy smile accentuated by her pose. It was Joan Sandfield on the cover, now perhaps the biggest blonde bombshell in

Hollywood. Jamie was jealous of Sandfield and heard rumors that her husband may have slept with the entertainer. It was not the first rumor about James Kelly and actresses. Some claimed that he had an affair with the most famous actress of all, who had died mysteriously about a year earlier.

"Did you screw her, James?" she crudely asked with her soft voice filled with sarcasm as she held up the magazine. The President was innocent. The two met at one time but nothing happened. However, that didn't matter; some people believed every rumor no matter how outlandish. He already discussed it with his wife, but Jamie was in the mood for a fight. Although he had plenty of dirt on his wife, which they both knew, the President decided to take the high ground.

"Let's not bring that up now, Jamie. We already talked about all of this before. I came up here to check on you." He found it interesting how she would go on the offensive when she in fact was the guilty party. So concerned about the frequency of his wife's infidelity was the President that he had paternity tests done on his two children. His daughter Cathy, the oldest, was nearly six, meaning the President had his doubts for some time. He suspected Jamie of playing around with other men almost as soon as the honeymoon ended, and later he discovered that she had been screwing movie stars and others. He secretly had some of his most trusted investigators gather the information for him about her indiscretions.

"You're not coming up here to check on me out of concern," she continued, starting to raise her voice. "I know what you are here to do. You're going to accuse me of faking sickness to avoid my *wifely duties*. You consider me a belonging, like some asset of your family. Meanwhile you're probably out banging some floozies!" Her voice was now becoming a yell.

"What are you talking about? Every President meets famous people, like entertainers and movie stars. Does that mean he's having sex with everyone he meets? Look at President Truman, he had Lauren Bacall sitting on top of the piano showing off her legs but nobody in the media accused him of having an affair." He stared back at her, trying to remain calm.

"I think you're playing around on me, James. And I'm getting tired of it. It's because of your behavior that I've had difficult pregnancies."

"Don't blame that on me!" He said as he began to raise his voice. The couple had lost three children: there was the miscarriage in 1955, a stillbirth in 1956, and their most recent child died shortly after birth just a few weeks earlier. The loss hurt him as much as it did his wife. "I told you not to listen to rumors. I don't know who is spreading them but they are not true! Don't trust the newspapers and media either. Don't you remember just before we became engaged the paper that tried to imply that I was gay? What did they base that on? Is it because I have a friend from college who is gay? I guess they use the same logic as you. If I'm friends with a gay man then I must be gay! If a female entertainer takes a picture with me then we must have had sex."

"There are rumors. I didn't hear rumors like that about any of the other Presidents. You know maybe I will divorce you anyway," she threatened as she angrily threw a pair of shoes against the back wall of her closet. She liked to use threats but he knew a divorce was unlikely, although with her instability he couldn't be sure. He felt she would divorce him eventually, but not until after the next election and, if he won, maybe not for another four years later. That is if she wanted the million dollars his father promised her. She loved money so it was pretty certain she wouldn't make any moves to lose out.

"You always make accusations and threats and it's getting old." He made a point not to sink to her level by bringing up any of her reckless and immoral trysts. And as for her trouble bearing healthy children, her addictive chain smoking and drinking during her pregnancies sure didn't help matters. No doubt, their losses were unfortunate and depressing for him too.

She stomped her feet violently in a childlike display. Circling the room like a bird of prey, she slammed the closet door as she passed it, then ran quickly into the bathroom and did the same with its door.

The President sighed loudly. After being greeted by Jamie's shouts of anger he now knew which of her personalities would appear behind the closed door. He thought to himself, *what did I do to deserve this? And why didn't I marry a helpful woman like Scott's wife?*

Chapter 23

Texas Hospitality

Early morning sun streamed through Ellen Lakeland's office windows. It was earlier still in Austin, but wheels were already in motion. The phone jangled, starting the day.

"President Kelly's office"

"Good morning Ellen, this is Governor Ron Conway in Texas. I'd like to speak with President Kelly, is he available?"

"Hello Governor Conway, let me put you on hold for a moment and I'll check to see if President Kelly is free to speak with you." The line went silent. Conway knew there was a good chance Kelly would avoid talking with him, even if he was available. The two put on a nice show in public, but since early 1961, when the Navy airplane carrying Red Farleigh crashed, their relationship was never the same. But politics being what it is, they both had to play along.

"Hello, Ron?"

"Good morning Mr. President. It's Ron Conway," the governor began in his best campaign voice. "I hate to bother you, but I have an important matter that's time sensitive and I need your help."

"What is it that you need, Ron?"

"Well, I know you have a trip to Texas planned in November; we talked about that in

Assassination Point Blank

June when you were down in El Paso with the Vice President and Clint Carson. I was hoping you could extend your stay a day or so longer to include Dallas. Members of the Party in the state requested I call you. We really need your diplomacy." There was a pause. "We can help each other bring Texas together and bring Texas home," the governor said poetically.

"Ron, I'd love to help, I really would. I'll have to check with my aides to see about my schedule," Kelly balked, not wanting to make a commitment on the spot.

"Sure, Mr. President, I wouldn't normally make such a request, but you're the only man that can bridge the divide between the two factions in the party," Conway implored.

"I understand your predicament," Kelly replied.

"And since you're going to be in Texas anyway I just thought it made sense," Conway continued to make his case. "I already spoke with Lionel, and he said it was a good idea and that you're welcome to join him at his ranch before you go back to Washington if you like. As a matter of fact, I'm flying to Washington today. I'll be there this afternoon. I tell you what, I'll stop by the White House, so we can go over it further," the governor said as if it was already a done deal.

"That sounds good Ron, I'll set aside some time to see you this afternoon," Kelly said. He knew Conway was right about one thing. He needed the electoral votes in Texas. If his schedule permitted, how could it hurt to spend an extra day in Texas?

***

In a dimly lit Washington watering hole, where the food is good, the service is discrete and privacy is at a premium, Governor Conway and Vice President Jones met for dinner. The two were seated at a corner table near the kitchen in a round high-backed leather booth.

"I got him to see the light," Ron Conway laughed proudly as he leaned back against the booth's burgundy colored leather bolsters.

"Didn't I tell you I'd make this happen!" he bragged to his long time buddy.

"I have to admit, you always come through Ronnie." Lionel cracked a rare smile, "we'll take good care of the boy when we get him down to Texas. That's OUR territory!" he bellowed slapping the table. Silverware jumped noisily.

Lionel enjoyed using the derogatory term "boy" when he referred to President Kelly behind his back.

The two men were dining at a restaurant well known to local politicians. The food was excellent and it was a noisy place, perfect for having private discourse in public. The roar of conversation echoed so deeply it was impossible to hear anything in particular at a distance of more than four feet.

"With all this heat coming down we need to get this thing done and soon."

"I know his brother is behind it," Lionel's eyes narrowed to slits, like a viper just before it strikes its prey. "And can you believe this Irish boy has the audacity to try and throw ME off his reelection ticket?" Lionel had heard the rumors. "Doesn't he know who he's dealing with?"

"Yeah, hard to believe isn't it," Conway agreed.

"How can a smart man be so stupid?"

"Well, too bad the Addison's disease hasn't killed him yet, but it sure looks like he has a death wish eh?" The Governor had obtained the President's medical records when Jones and Kelly were running against each other in the primaries for the Democratic nomination.

"He thinks I can be fired?" Lionel growled. Even with the loud background noise, the governor instinctively looked around to see if anyone was listening.

Governor Conway knew that his mentor had far more serious concerns than being removed from the presidential ticket. The Vice President had two major crises brewing for years that had now reached their boiling point and needed to be solved quickly.

One was his Texas business partner, Willy Eastman who was indicted the year before on a multitude of fraud charges, including some related to illegal purchases of agriculture allotments and another scandal involving mortgages and fertilizer tanks. Although Willy Eastman was one of his major financial backers, Lionel wouldn't let the man's indictment lead to his downfall. Willy might have to be sacrificed. Lionel recommended a lawyer for his friend. Unbeknownst to Eastman, the lawyer was a man who would protect *Lionel's* interests first and prepare Willy's defense second. But even that buffer might not be enough for Jones.

Lionel's second problem was right before his eyes in Washington and even more far-reaching. It involved his longtime political advisor in the Senate, Buddy Burns. For twenty years Burns worked in the Senate and had ridden Lionel's coattails, cutting deals for both his boss and himself whenever feasible. As Secretary to the Majority leader, Burns had become so powerful in his own right that he was considered the "101st senator," the second most powerful man in the Senate after Lionel. Senators knew that if they wanted to accomplish anything in DC, they had to go through Lionel Jones and that meant dealing with Buddy.

But all good things eventually come to an end and so it was with Buddy Burns. Burns was smart enough to rise quickly but not thorough enough to cover his tracks. Just the month before, in September of 1963, the chickens of his shady business deals were finally coming home to roost. The Republicans had launched an investigation into his business and political activities. Among a host of other allegations, Burns was under investigation for a company he established which received lucrative government contracts. The company had links to Lionel Jones and other important people in Washington – and with a number of figures known well in the world of organized crime.

Naturally Burn's trouble was quickly becoming Lionel's. If the investigations into these scandals continued it could end his political career or even lead to criminal prosecution. Seeing this as a possibility, for the past couple of years Jones and Conway were not sitting still. They had seen potential trouble coming over a year earlier and efforts were made to gain counterintelligence on the President and his brother. The previous summer, Conway's former son-in-law, whose nickname was Papa Pioneer, broke into a woman's apartment in Los Angeles. The woman, Justine Exford, was known to be a message courier between the President and an organized crime figure in Chicago who was working with the CIA. Two days prior to Papa Pioneer's apartment break-in, a second female information courier, also in Los Angeles, was found dead in her home. The second woman was a famous Hollywood actress and foul play was suspected. Was the star's death designed to frame the Attorney General and a method of killing two birds with one stone? If so, it nearly worked. But it didn't, and now Lionel and Conway were forced to play their old trump card.

One thing Ron Conway had learned in working for his mentor over the years was that, like a wounded animal, when Lionel Jones was cornered and threatened he could be dangerous. And the twin scandals he now faced involving Buddy Burns and Willy Eastman were like two steel sides of a trap closing down. The current dilemma was similar to past confrontations he had in Texas, only greater in size and more complicated. But if the past was any indication of the future, things were about to get messy.

"Angler will fill you in on everything when you meet. He wants you to coordinate a lot of it," Lionel explained, looking up from his bloody plate. He liked his beef rare. "This has to go down flawlessly, you understand?" It wasn't a request, it was an order. As one of Lionel's most trusted assets, Conway was being placed front and center, underscoring the seriousness of Lionel's troubles. He was always a high stakes kind of guy and wanted Kelly removed as much as anyone. He relished his coming role but he was curious about the operation.

"Did you talk with Harvey?" Conway inquired, referring to Harvey Hampton, the FBI director.

"Yes, he's in. We've got it all arranged." It was a dumb question but he had to ask anyway. Lionel and Harvey Hampton were very close. For almost twenty years, the two men lived less than 200 feet apart. They often met for breakfast and took walks together. Lionel promised Hampton that once he became president he would pass an executive order allowing Hampton to have the Director's job for life. As it was now he would have to retire soon – he was nearing the mandatory retirement age of 70. With Harvey leading the investigation, the evidence would be maneuvered in such a way that it would point to a fall guy.

"What about the Secret Service?" Conway probed, wanting to get more information from

Lionel. He knew the Secret Service was as important for the operation's success as the FBI.

"We have a few minor details to be handled, but they're with us too," Lionel said chewing a piece of red fatty rib roast. "For a lot of reasons many of them are not too happy with the President and his brother. For one thing they fear their agency will be taken from the Department of the Treasury and placed under the FBI," he explained swallowing a large piece of meat. Then in a low heartless voice he leaned in, "Listen Ron, nobody likes this boy. And nobody's going to care when he dies. He's got a lot of enemies." Conway knew what Lionel meant. Many common folks might be fond of President Kelly, but that wasn't going to matter. Those in charge of the aftermath and its investigation didn't mind if the man got whacked. In fact, many were cheerfully anticipating how much they stood to benefit. Still, Conway was curious about the particulars of the mission.

"That's good. But what about…" Lionel cut him off.

"You're asking too many goddamn questions!" Lionel hollered losing his patience. "After you meet with Angler you're going to know more than anyone," he lowered his voice as he leaned in, "you just take care of your end and the rest will be handled. You got that?"

"I understand. I'll get the job done, Lionel. I'll take care of whatever needs to be done. I'm all in, you know that," he said confidently. "But you've got to make sure I come out of this smelling like a rose," Conway beseeched. At that moment the Vice President knew as always he could count on his wily friend. He smiled with satisfaction. Beneath the veneer, the Governor was an unconscious risk taker. He realized that Conway had no compunction about executing his role, nor was he getting nosy, it was simply nervous excitement. Conway merely wanted to make sure that others were onboard.

"Ron, relax we've got your back covered. My God, trust me, you're going to come outta this smelling better than a Texas Rose when we get through. That much I guarantee," Lionel laughed. Conway's ruthlessness and cunning were the qualities Lionel loved about the man. He was useful and could leave more dead bodies in the field with less remorse than any politician Lionel ever met. "Bob Angler will brief you before you head back to Austin. And the night before, we'll have a meeting to tie up loose ends. I didn't mean to snap at you Ron. You've done a lot for me. I haven't forgotten it. Now let's enjoy our meal."

Chapter 24

The Lone Star and the First Lady of Texas

"I'm telling you Milly, that son of a bitch and his brother are out to ruin Lionel," complained Big Ron Conway to his wife. "Do you know what that means?"

"I can't stand him, honey. He has no business being President of the United States," replied his wife, sipping her morning coffee. "Our good friend Lionel Jones should have gotten the nomination. Then maybe you could have been vice president," she smiled. "Why Lionel ever went on the ticket with Kelly I'll never know."

"Well, he's behind it and creating a lot of problems, that's for damn sure," the governor replied in his slow Texas drawl. "But can you believe the nerve - that they would be investigating a good honest Texan like Lionel?"

"No. Those Catholics have certainly lost their minds, coming down to this clean part of the country and stirring up so much trouble. It was bad enough when you found out that they plan to throw Lionel off the ticket. Do they think he's like a used part on an automobile that they can just toss in the junkyard and keep on motoring? This is so horrible, Ron. Lionel and Raven are the nicest people and they've been so good to us."

"Dear, it's even worse. These guys are on an all out rampage. Right down here in own back yard. The audacity! And they won't stop until they strip Lionel of his political office and put him in jail. And after that, since we're good friends, you can bet they'll be on us too," the Governor said studying his wife. "No way they're going to stop with Lionel and Raven." He could see his wife getting upset. The Governor knew how to push her buttons. She was normally very refined, sweet and in control, the perfect wife of a politician, but when threatened she had a mean streak. When provoked she could be more ruthless than her husband.

"That's right, Milly" he continued. "They plan to take everything away from us too. Everything we've worked for."

"Over my dead body they will!" Milly interrupted, her voice rising, her eyes narrowing to slits as her face became red. She stopped herself. "Didn't you and Lionel discuss what you're going to do about this, Ron?" she implored.

"Yes, we did. We have a solution. And I'm glad you understand the seriousness of what's at stake because it looks like we're going to need your help." He studied her momentarily, already knowing her answer.

"What? What is it you want me to do?" She looked up and could now see the confidence on her husband's face. She knew he and Lionel would come out on top. He was merely stressing the importance of the situation and that he needed her. "Anything, just name it, Ron. It would be my pleasure to help you gentlemen."

"I knew I could count on you, Milly. A good woman can lift a man up or bring him down," he smiled. "You're my lovely Texas rose. That's why you'll always be my first lady."

Chapter 25

Cruising the Greek Isles Oct '63

In early October of 1963, Jamie Kelly left the United States to cruise the Greek Isles aboard Arion Ostratos' yacht. It had been surprisingly easy to persuade her husband that she should go. They lost a newborn baby two months before, and both of them had spiraled into depression. It was the third child she had lost in the ten years of marriage. The President was terribly saddened over his son's death, and immersed himself in his busy schedule as a distraction from the grievous event.

Jamie didn't have the same kind of distractions, and her sorrow was overwhelming. Life moved on, and it felt as if neither she nor the baby had mattered at all. She wore her grief as an accusation. She acted haughty and antisocial. Friends suggested that a vacation might be therapeutic for her. Perhaps they were correct, he thought. He acquiesced. She was acting surly and recalcitrant recently anyway; so what harm could it do? It wasn't the first time she traveled without him. Just the year before, she visited India with her sister Leslie. Now Leslie had invited her on a cruise with Ostratos, and it seemed to be a perfect opportunity for everyone to get a break.

Assassination Point Blank

Ostratos, one of the wealthiest men in the world, had made his official fortune in shipping and airlines - and unorthodox endeavors such as whaling off the coast of South America. He had also made an unofficial fortune in drug trafficking, decades before the formation of the CIA.

The man was world famous for his wealth and mystique - and for his romances with high-profile women, many of whom were married. One was Jamie's sister, Princess Leslie Radzinger. Leslie and her husband, Prince Stewart Radzinger, were also on the cruise. Theirs had been an "open marriage" from the beginning four years earlier, and they socialized often with Ostratos. Leslie was currently Ostratos's favorite, and he showered her with lavish gifts. According to some it was only a matter of time before the two would marry. She would divorce her husband in a heartbeat to live an exciting life aboard Arion's yacht and private island, if he proposed.

But to Ostratos Leslie was already a past conquest; he had taken her to bed on numerous occasions, and even bragged jokingly to his friends about what it was like to screw a Princess. But now his eyes were on a new, more challenging prize: her sister, the first lady of the United States, America's Queen. Ostratos was a masterful poker player; nobody ever knew precisely what he was thinking. Indeed, he was a charmer, but he could turn on you like a cobra.

When an opportunity presented itself he took advantage by inviting Jamie Kelly for a relaxing cruise aboard his giant yacht, the *Aphrodite*, supposedly to relieve her depression.

The White House simply announced that the First Lady would be spending the first two weeks of October in Greece to rest and vacation. The public was fully aware of the sadness of her loss so it was not surprising. However, there was no mention in the announcement that Jamie would in fact be aboard Ostratos' luxurious vessel.

★★★

"Welcome aboard," Arion Ostratos said, as he cheerfully greeted his guests. He was dressed in an olive green Italian silk suit. His hair was slicked back and combed neatly in place. To say he looked like a million bucks was an understatement. The first lady smiled back as she ascended the last few feet of the steep ramp attached to the prodigious vessel. Two of her Secret Service Agents, Cliff Hillman and Pete Landry followed close behind.

"Hello Arion, thank you so much for your gracious invitation. It is wonderful to see you again. What a beautiful ship, it's so large!" she exclaimed as she removed her dark glasses. She was impressed with the breathtaking vessel. Who wouldn't be?

Yeah, I know, I have a bigger one than your husband, he snickered to himself. James Kelly's 92-foot vessel was imposingly luxurious, but even it could not compare with Arion's 325-foot yacht.

Arion turned to Jamie. "Allow me to give you and your agents a tour of the ship," he said graciously, knowing full well that Jamie Kelly had been on the ship years ago. "The other guests have all seen the ship at one time or another so they know their way around." Ostratos stood admiring the first lady from head to toe for a moment. She was only 36 - more than twenty-five years his junior - and she wore her sadness like a veil. It accentuated her elegance.

"That would be wonderful, Mr. Ostratos."

"Call me Arion, please. You're here to relax and have a good time. First names are in order. Let me start by saying it's an honor to have you aboard," he said taking her hand for a moment. "I'll show you around," he said as one of his servants followed closely. He had a quick wit and had traveled all over the world. To say he was part of the jet set was an understatement. He *owned* the jet set. No woman could resist being enchanted.

"Take a look at the swimming pool," he said with a smile as they moved from the main deck's atrium toward the pool. "It's salt water. In the evening the cover serves as a dance floor as well. It has a mosaic bottom," Arion pointed downward. The bottom of the pool was adorned with tiles of different colors carefully arranged to create a beautiful work of art.

"It's a Minotaur. What a great idea. I love it!" Jamie said admiring the beauty of mosaic art on the floor of the pool.

"On this deck is the main dining room, where we will have our meals. There's also a bar and two lounges, one is specifically for music. Some of the guest cabins are on this deck down the hall," he pointed. "I have sailboats and a cruise boat to go to land if we need it for shallow waters. I have a crew of 58 onboard to tend to all your needs, including a Swedish masseuse and two hairdressers from Paris, so don't worry about the wind in your hair," he laughed.

"So this is what it is like to be a king," Jamie said softly, overwhelmed by the ships opulence.

"What do you gentlemen think of my boat?" He asked, eyeballing Hillman and Landry for a moment.

"It's a truly magnificent ship, Mr. Ostratos," Landry replied awed.

"It's incredible. I've never seen anything like it, sir." Hillman added.

Arion Ostratos smiled at their enthusiasm. "Thank you gentlemen, I appreciate the compliments. I hope you enjoy the cruise." He turned to the first lady, "Carlos will show you to your cabins. If you need anything let Carlos know. This afternoon I have some business to attend to so I will be occupied, but I will join you this evening for dinner."

Hillman and Landry marveled at the size and beauty of the ship and its ornate furnishings.

The amenities aboard *The Aphrodite* were eye-popping. Every room had something special. The bar had stools upholstered in whale skin. In the game room there were card tables and handcrafted playing boards for chess, checkers, and backgammon enthusiasts. There was a spa, a library, a showroom, a playroom for children, and even a landing pad for Ostratos' helicopter. Hillman looked at Landry with a wide-eyed expression that said, *Wow! Some people sure do know how to live.*

Ostratos made a point to show the first lady his cabin suite and lounge. After touring *The Aphrodite,* Ostratos could sense Jamie's fascination. He had become one of the wealthiest men in the world for several reasons; one was his intuition. By the look in her eye he knew Jamie Kelly would be returning to his cabin suite before the end of the cruise. It turned him on to think that he could buy just about anything in the world, including the First Lady of the United States. Ostratos was pragmatic; everyone had a price, even Jamie Kelly. What made his pursuit of her even more thrilling was that he detested her brother-in-law, Scott Kelly, and knew her mere presence on his yacht was making his blood boil. From the time they met ten years earlier, the two men despised each other. Ostratos blamed Scott Kelly for the failure of one of his business ventures. Rumors, misinformation, and plain paranoia increased the tension.

Carlos showed the first lady and her agents to their cabins. Their luggage was already delivered to their rooms by Ostratos's servants. Despite the man's wolfish charm and impressive possessions, Cliff Hillman couldn't help but wonder if behind Ostratos's glittery facade was still an insecure gangster. The man's physical appearance made the thought even more compelling. Clearly Ostratos would never make it as a Secret Service Agent Hillman thought, laughing to himself. He was short, dark and toad-like in appearance, but even Hillman had to admit the little tycoon did have enormous charisma. Observing him flirting with Jamie Kelly and her reciprocating interest in the man's mystique made him a bit jealous. The disparaging thoughts helped him feel secure around the rich, powerful man.

The other guests, thirteen in total, including Jamie's sister Leslie and her husband, were already aboard in their cabins. Arion's older sister and her husband came along as well. Also joining the group was Mr. & Mrs. Rose, who were mutual friends of both Arion and the Kelly family. On the cruise, Mr. Rose was instructed by Scott Kelly to keep an eye on Jamie and Ostratos in an effort to make sure nothing occurred that shouldn't. Of course Mr. Rose realized this was an impossible task if two consenting parties wanted to sneak off together. What was he supposed to do? Especially since Ostratos owned the vessel. Even so, Scott Kelly figured that since he and the President could not stop Jamie from going on the trip, at least they could have an extra set of eyes onboard which might keep Ostratos's behavior in check.

For the first two days Ostratos strategically kept a low profile. During the day he attended to business in his cabin suite and private area only joining his guests for evening meals. Nevertheless over dinner he sensed the first lady's interest. She stayed up late, captivated by his stories. She listened intently as he mentioned how he spent millions converting *The Aphrodite* from a military vessel to a state of the art luxury cruising yacht that made all others, even those in the richest ports of the Mediterranean, gaze at it with envy. He found her sexy and provocative.

On the third evening of the cruise Ostratos joined his guests for some elaborate French cuisine, but this time the dining room was decorated in a cozy, romantic fashion. The lights were dimmed and the table was decorated with candles. While romantic music played in the background, Ostratos talked about his exceptional life. He proved to be a wonderful storyteller. Over dinner he described to his guests how he narrowly escaped the genocide in Turkey with only the shirt on his back and left for Buenos Aires aboard a ship. In Argentina he founded a tobacco import company and began manufacturing his own cigarette line, which focused on women consumers. He parlayed his tobacco fortune into shipping and airlines to become a modern day Odysseus. His life story was an alchemy of sex, money, power, fame, and mystery. Even Jamie's secret service men were entertained listening to the man's biography. They also found it amusing to see how the help onboard stood at attention and came running to Ostratos's side whenever he snapped his fingers. When he was angry or tipsy from wine he might hiss at the help like a snake, but on this trip he was in a good mood. Ostratos's intentions did not escape everyone at the table.

Seeing Ostratos's fondness of her sister gave Leslie misgivings about having invited Jamie on the cruise. Tension filled the air as bitter sibling competition once again raised its ugly head. Like her sister, Leslie was unhappy with her marriage. Rich, powerful, charismatic, and generous, Arion Ostratos seemed to both sisters to be the perfect escape plan and solution.

From the beginning Leslie had been in competition with his other mistress, the most famous opera singer in the world, who Ostratos showed off to the world like a Rembrandt or Picasso. At the peak of that relationship, Ostratos's first wife, and mother of his children, was so mortified that she ended the marriage. She didn't mind that Arion was a playboy but to have him on the front page of newspapers around the world with his opera singer mistress was too much. As costly as that relationship had been, Arion had thrown over his songbird for the princess. Leslie hoped this meant his intentions with her were, if not honorable, certainly serious. Now, just when Leslie was breaking through she made a fatal mistake. She found some consolation. Her sister was married as well, to the President of the United States no less.

"Would anybody care to dance this evening? After dessert I can have the musicians play," Ostratos informed his guests at the table as he looked at Jamie. He was an accomplished dancer, having spent so much of his youth making a name for himself in the tango clubs of Buenos Aires.

"Arion that sounds fabulous," Jamie replied in her soft voice, her eyes sparkling. Stu Radzinger noticed the unmistakable chemistry between Ostratos and Jamie. The first lady listened intently and showed obvious interest in Arion. The two were hitting it off. Being more sensitive and observant than most men, Stu could feel the tension of sibling rivalry in the air. He knew too well about his wife's insecurities and how throughout her youth she played second fiddle to her sister in the competition for their father's attention. He looked down and out of the corner of his eye he detected movement in his wife's lap. Her hands were tightly clenched fists twisting her napkin around as if it were a wet bath towel in need of a good wringing. He looked at his wife's face and could discern the jealousy and sadness at having lost another competitive battle to Jamie.

In exchange for sharing his beautiful wife with Ostratos, Stu was rewarded with a place on the board of directors of Ostratos's airline. In an odd paradox he felt bad that, as in their childhood, his wife once again fell short to her older sister and might be thrown aside by the playboy. As the evening wore on it was obvious to Stu that Ostratos intended to make Jamie his new mistress. He wondered if it was his imagination running wild but he couldn't shake the feeling that Ostratos and Jamie would end up together. *Would the man ever marry again? But why should he? He loved the playboy lifestyle,* thought Stu.

Playing one woman off another was just another cunning Machiavellian technique used by Ostratos. He already had one but he was determined to have both sisters.

While the orchestra played Ostratos danced with Jamie.

"Are you having a nice time?" he asked pensively.

"Oh, it's wonderful Mr. Ostratos, I mean Arion," she said correcting herself.

"How was your dinner?"

"French cuisine is my favorite. It was delicious," she responded starry eyed.

"I have chefs from Greece, Italy, and France, can't go wrong with that when it comes to food can you?" he said looking at her as they slow danced to a song Ostratos told the orchestra to play.

"I know it's been a difficult time for you. I'm delighted you could come on the cruise."

"I wouldn't have missed it for the world."

They continued to dance. As the song came to its end Ostratos said, "When you can slip away later this evening, meet me in the lounge."

Assassination Point Blank

"I look forward to it," she nodded seductively as they left the dance floor. It wouldn't be the first time Jamie played around on her husband. Despite the media's favorable portrayal of her, she could be a bad girl; once she cheated on her husband with a movie star in a Cold Water Canyon mansion.

There were men with money and men who knew how to entertain and have a good time. Arion Ostratos was both, Jamie thought dreamily as she left the dance floor. *The Aphrodite* and Arion were just her style. First class all the way. The finest dining, servants, every amenity one could imagine. She took advantage of the pampering, even having her bed sheets changed twice daily. It suited her. She felt better than she had in a long time.

***

Later that evening, as *The Aphrodite* cruised southward through the wine colored waters of the Ionian Sea toward Ithaca, Jamie quietly left her cabin to rendezvous with Arion. He was already waiting for her in his dimly lit bar next to the lounge. The lights were turned down and it took her eyes a few seconds to adjust to the darkness of the room. With a bright smile he rose from his stool. At the same time his bartender came over.

"What will you have to drink Madam?"

"A martini would be delightful," she replied opening her purse in search of a cigarette.

"Excellent choice."

A few moments later the bartender placed a martini glass filled to the rim and a small cup of green olives in front of her.

"Arion, tell me the whole story behind *The Aphrodite*," Jamie requested, wide-eyed.

"I bought the vessel for scrap value, but I've put millions into it," he said.

Ten years earlier the ship belonged to the Royal Canadian Navy, but he converted it to a luxury yacht. He spent millions in making it "the last word in luxury." Aboard the vessel the smell of saline, sex, and opulence coupled with wealth, power, and Mediterranean romance seduced some of the most beautiful women of the world.

"And what did you do when you left Europe for Argentina?" she asked.

"When the Turks seized my village, I was forced to leave. Several of my uncles were murdered and their property taken." He looked at her with sorrow in his eyes. "First I worked some odd jobs. One was on the night shift at a telephone company. Then I started importing tobacco and that's when I started my own cigarette company, with marketing targeted toward women smokers." Arion conveniently did not mention his father's help in the tobacco business, since the two men had a falling out. Nor did he discuss another secret to his success: his dabbling in drug trafficking, using his tobacco imports as a cover. It was a rich source of extra income and helped to launch his shipping business.

"You've had such a fascinating life," Jamie said earnestly.

"You make it sound like it's over," he joked.

"No, I didn't mean that…"

"I know," he said laughing. "Earlier today I showed you my private island and told you about my life and adventures. I'd like to hear more about yours," he inquired. "After all it's not every day I have an icon of Washington on my ship," he said half joking. Jamie knew full well the celebrities who cruised with Arion. His directness was refreshing. From the beginning she felt at ease. He treated her like a real person, not an object or a celebrity to be worshipped or gawked upon. He had been around the rich and famous and was not intimidated by looks, fame or money. She instantly found herself attracted to the mysterious and dangerous qualities of the Greek; he reminded her of her father. Even his dark hair and complexion was similar – only Arion was infinitely wealthier. Early in the day he had given her a tour of the orchards, vineyards, and beaches he created on his private island. He turned the nearly barren island into a paradise. Perhaps it was her sadness of losing a child or simply the exhilaration of The Aphrodite but at that moment she longed to stay with Ostratos forever.

"Let's move to the lounge next door, it's more comfortable there," he said.

Assassination Point Blank

After several martinis Jamie and Ostratos began to kiss. He ran his hand up her leg. She enjoyed it.

"Are you going to take me to your cabin?" she asked. He could see the lust in her eyes.

"Any time you're ready," he replied. As he spoke she rose from the couch.

***

What difference does it make? Jamie asked herself the next morning while lying in Arion's large bed. She contemplated her promiscuous behavior and justified it by accusing her husband of the same. If some details of her cruise on Ostratos's yacht did happen to circulate in the press, it might cost her husband the election. So be it. That would cut their marriage short. Amen. She would no longer have to endure four more years with him.

She harbored irrational resentment and she was more reckless since the recent death of her child. She was visiting a hypnotherapist to help with her depression. After college she worked with the CIA on a special project and they explained that her high intelligence and wide-set eyes made her an ideal candidate for hypnosis. The various projects involving hypnosis were supposed to help her forget traumatic events like the loss of three children.

Through a glass doorway she could see Arion dressed in a white robe, its brightness highlighted by the morning sun. He stood on the balcony of his bedroom looking out at the island of Ithaca. Jamie came out to join him.

Assassination Point Blank

It was a beautiful sunny day. She was mystified when she saw the scowl on his face.

"Is something wrong?"

"See that ship over there?" he pointed demonstratively at a large vessel across the harbor.

"Yes"

"That's one of my brother-in-law's cargo ships, or I should say my former brother-in-law, the dirty bastard!"

"Spiros Nucchios?"

"Yes, that son of a bitch slept with my ex-wife, his wife's sister!" Arion's capacity to hate at times overwhelmed him.

So that's what is bothering him, Jamie thought. She knew the story. Spiros she heard was as much of a playboy as Arion but he was more unassuming. Despite his criticism of Nucchios, Ostratos was mirroring his rival's behavior as he courted two married sisters onboard his yacht. The two shipping tycoons despised each other, perhaps because they were so much alike.

Ostratos had many rivals in business but perhaps none was more personal and ugly than this one with his brother-in-law, Spiros Nucchios.

"That son of a bitch has been a thorn in my side for years," a frown appeared. "He's trying to ruin me, just like Scott Kelly," he muttered under his breath. Then a slight smile appeared. It made him feel good to know that having gotten the first lady in bed he had put one over on Scotty Kelly. Only two things were better than sex; one was getting Scott Kelly upset and the other was getting even.

***

The phone rang. Demitri Grabos answered.

"Hello,"

"I had her last night," Arion boasted over the static of an overseas telephone line to his longtime friend and business partner.

"That's great Arion," Grabos said, not quite sure how to respond to his friend's immature behavior.

"Don't worry, she's not in the room. She's out by the pool. I'll bet the little Irishman will be redder than a beet when he sees it in the newspapers," laughed Ostratos, referring to Scott Kelly.

"Actually I hope it doesn't get in the papers, Arion. I don't like him any more than you but I'm not sure this is a good thing." The two men were close, like brothers. However, at this critical juncture, Grabos wanted Arion to focus more on business instead of pleasure.

"Demitri, you worry too much. You're a worrier, that's your problem," Arion said making light of Grabos's concerns.

"Maybe so, but remember we still have that project in Haiti that hasn't finalized."

Grabos was referring to Ostratos's ambitious plans with the President of Haiti to upgrade the port, build a refinery, and a casino, explore for commodities inland, and transform the country into a vacation resort like Monaco. Ostratos would receive more favorable tax deals if he registered his ships under the Haitian flag. Grabos was concerned it could be undermined, as had happened to Arion's Saudi oil transport deal ten years earlier, if Ostratos attracted too much attention in the newspapers with the first lady onboard. Despite the careful planning and brilliance of the project, Grabos had a bad feeling. He had put in a lot of time for Arion in negotiating and planning the project. There was no doubt Arion was a genius when it came to business, but lately he was overly obsessed with melodrama and it frustrated Demitri. He wanted Arion regain his old drive and focus for business.

"Yeah, I know all that Demitri," Arion said trying to calm his friend's apprehension. "It'll all work out, you'll see. We'll go down to Haiti soon and talk to the president. Oh, and I almost forgot, have you heard from Jeffrey lately?" Arion was asking about Jeffrey Morganson, a Russian geologist and one of their business associates involved in the project.

"The last time I spoke with him he was in Haiti. He's been there since June." Static was breaking in between their words.

"Listen, our connection is not good. We'll talk more when I get back home, alright? And we'll get down to Haiti. Ciao"

"Goodbye Arion."

Demitri hung up the phone. He got to thinking more about Morganson, their "geologist" for the Haiti project. In his day, Grabos had come across many colorful and enigmatic characters, but something about Morganson's shadowy past nagged at him. The two

Greeks first met the mysterious man in 1961 at a dinner party in Panama. Morganson, originally from Russia, was ubiquitous and seemed to know everyone, including the first lady, her sister, and her mother Janet. Some digging revealed that years ago he was very close to Janet, presumably even her lover before she married Herman, an heir to the Standard oil fortune. Jamie and Leslie knew Morganson from the time they were small children, even calling him "Uncle Jeff." Those associations furthered Arion's interest. He decided to bring Morganson aboard the project to help explore for oil and other natural resources in Haiti. Skeptical, Grabos pondered whether Morganson was the best candidate for the enterprise. Arion reassured him, saying again not to worry, that in addition to being a scientist, Morganson spoke many languages and was known to have unlimited contacts in the CIA and other intelligence communities throughout the world, which would be of further benefit to them in Haiti.

His intuition also told him there was nothing necessarily evil about Morganson, but the secrecy surrounding the refined Russian and his ability to be all things to all people, like a chameleon, made Grabos uncomfortable. Between the strange geologist, Arion's volatile personality, and love triangles, Demitri couldn't help but worry about the project's future.

Chapter 26

Spiros Nucchios

On the patio of his opulent Parisian villa, Spiros Nucchios lunched with his long time associate Connor Elman. They sat in the autumn sun wearing light coats due to the cool air. Olives and wine sat on a nearby table.

"I understand Scott Kelly was more upset than the president when he heard the news," said Connor Elman, a large disarming southerner who also happened to be a CIA spymaster. He and Nucchios had been exchanging information for years. "The little Irishman is furious about his sister-in-law going on that cruise," Connor smiled.

"This is going even better than I thought," Spiros said with satisfaction.

"There's nothing more enjoyable than watching two of our enemies fighting, blinded by anger, huh?" Connor said in his barely detectible southern accent. "The two despise each other and there's nothing worse than having a pretty woman between two men. They're not like you Spiros, they're intelligent men but they can't keep their egos in check."

"Something that started out as mere conflicting personalities has managed to grow into a vendetta," Nucchios thought, amazed at what a little misinformation could do to exacerbate a situation. Behind the scenes the CIA deceived Ostratos into thinking Scott Kelly was indeed out to get him. And he believed it! Then Ostratos escalated matters by becoming involved with Leslie and now inviting the first lady onboard his yacht.

"A few years ago I too was a little worried about the American," Spiros said, reflecting on the past. The bad blood all started about ten years earlier when the branch of the government Scott Kelly worked in, the Internal Security Section was investigating Soviet agents. Kelly began investigating Greek shipping families in New York for trading with the enemy, Red China, while the US was fighting the communists in Korea. Although he had no ships involved in the trade with China, Ostratos feared that it would make his company more visible at a time when he sought to remain low profile because he was working on a behemoth oil tanker transport contract with Saudi Arabia.

The deal with the Saudis collapsed and Ostratos invariably blamed Scott Kelly for it, even though Kelly was not actually targeting him. He became wary of Scott Kelly. His suspicion grew to full blown paranoia and a conviction that the ambitious young American was out to ruin him. Hiding in the shadows, Spiros Nucchios and Elman's CIA were the ones in fact behind much of his trouble.

Nucchios and Ostratos had been fierce competitors for decades. And although Arion had obtained more headlines, Spiros had won important battles behind the scenes. It was he

Assassination Point Blank

who secretly sabotaged Arion's agreement with the Royal family of Saudi Arabia which would have allowed Ostratos to have exclusive contracts to transport all the oil out of the kingdom. Nucchios realized the ramifications and reported his findings to his powerful contacts inside the CIA. A coalition of influential men inside the government of the United States mobilized and sank Ostratos's dream. The oil executives and CIA officials met with powerful people in Washington and brought heavy pressure and threats on the House of Saud, forcing them to renege on their deal. Worst of all for Ostratos, he never discovered who was behind the information leak. As a result of his tip, Nucchios gained more powerful allies and weakened his competition.

Nucchios not only interfered with Arion's business deals, he also had an affair with Arion's wife. In fact, that is how he discovered the Saudi agreement. Had the deal worked out, Arion would have become more powerful than most countries. The failure was a major blow. Spin doctors in the CIA deflected Ostratos's attention away from Nucchios. He blamed Scott Kelly for his failures, unable to understand that Spiros Nucchios and his symbiotic relationship with the CIA were in fact the cause of his trouble.

"Spiros, I think this could be the beginning of the end for both the little turtle and those Irishmen in Washington," Connor said.

"A Greek tragedy? Let's hope so." Spiros Nucchios wasn't sure exactly how it would all end, but he felt secure knowing he was in good standing with the CIA for his exchange of the most valuable commodity of all – information. He was considered one of the CIA's best assets in Greece. Connor's old boss, Albert Diller, the former director of the CIA, held Nucchios in the highest regard. Still, he was under no illusion, he understood that the CIA could be for and against one at the same time. He was fully aware that the Kelly brothers were mortal enemies of the CIA, and that Ostratos was unpredictable. Hotheaded and stubborn, Ostratos could present a problem for them at any given time; it was his nature. If at times he proved useful, the CIA might use Ostratos, but he wouldn't last. Nucchios knew one day he'd be thrown to the sharks.

Chapter 27

Back on Arion's Love Boat

When *The Aphrodite* made port at Istanbul, Stu Radzinger was ready to fly home. Although he was polite while on the cruise, he had seen enough of Arion making points with Jamie. Observing the love triangle and competitiveness of the sisters for Arion's attention soured the mood. As he gathered his belongings in his cabin he tried to forget about the perverted situation. He needed to get back to the mainland.

"Are you sure you want to leave?" Leslie asked her husband.

"Yes, I'm sure. I've seen enough," his ambiguity failed to hide his sarcasm.

"Ha, ha I know what you're talking about," Leslie retorted with obvious irritation. She knew her sister was winning again.

"I have things to do back home."

"Like what?" she mocked him, taking her frustrations out on him.

"I have some work to do," he said diplomatically.

"So you're going to leave me here playing second fiddle?"

She had a way of twisting a situation around, only seeing it from her point of view, never placing herself in his shoes. She must have learned it from her sister, Stu thought. He always felt that Jamie was a bad influence on his wife. Most of his wife's faults came from trying to compete with her older sister.

"I didn't invite her. Put yourself in my shoes. I don't like seeing this any more than you. I will leave you with this thought; you would do well to remember how Arion discarded the opera singer."

"You're crazy!" she snapped.

"Am I?" he answered coolly. "You two have been fighting over the same men since you were babies, starting with your father! She always wins and you always end up hurt," he continued not wanting to escalate the argument but he didn't like seeing his wife humiliated once again by her sister. "I may not be a genius but at least I'm smart enough to get off this crazy ship."

"You think Arion is going to leave me for Jamie? Have you forgotten that my sister is the First Lady of the United States?" she reminded him as if the world were a static place. "There's a million dollars at stake," she added.

"Think whatever you want. I'm going back home." He hit a nerve. It was unintended but inevitable. It was impossible to have a logical conversation; she was too emotionally invested with Arion.

Thankfully his premature exit would not attract much attention from the others onboard since Arion had told his guests if they needed to leave the cruise early they could do so when the ship stopped at various ports.

As he packed his belongings into his suitcase he pondered his marital situation. It was his third marriage. He had to admit at times he wasn't the easiest person to get along with either. He loved his wife but he was realistic enough to know that being nearly twenty years older than her his best days were behind him and that at some point his pretty wife would trade up for another man. She was too ambitious for the status quo. As insanely twisted as her affair with Arion was, if she were to leave him he would prefer it to be with the legendary man, a man who had helped him in the business world. It would at least be understandable. But now, thanks to Jamie, it looked like that might not happen. Arion clearly wanted the first lady.

Maybe Leslie was right, the two could not marry right away but there was no denying what he saw. Wild thoughts raced through his mind. Jamie could become Arion's new mistress. He could see it. The relationship could intensify, especially the following year if James Kelly lost the presidential election. He marveled at how Jamie could hide behind a Madonna smile while doing something cruel to her sister.

Through his wife Stu knew all about Jamie's unhappiness in her marriage and about the threats of divorce she levied against the Kelly family. She had leverage and she used it. The threats were egregious but still serious enough that the old patriarch William Kelly intervened and promised her a million dollars to stay married. *The old man sure knows how to handle sticky situations,* Stu thought. Of course in this case with the rich Ostratos, what was a million dollars? The Greek owned several large companies, and had virtual control over a city-state principality in the south of France. He had his own island, for heaven's sake. If Leslie was considering leaving him, why would it be crazy to think Jamie might have entertained the same line of thinking? The more he pondered the possibilities surrounding Ostratos and Jamie Kelly the more he realized he wasn't crazy. He was onto something.

***

"I don't understand her thinking going on that playboy's ship," a disgusted Scott Kelly said, red-faced as he flung the morning paper on the President's desk. A picture of Arion Ostratos, the first lady, and Leslie abroad Arion's yacht took up half a page. "This is what I was worried about. Talk about frustrating!"

"I'm not happy about it either Scott, but there's not much we can do now," the President replied. "You know how she gets. Once she received the invitation from Leslie, there was no dissuading her. She was so upset about the baby..." He stopped, trying to collect himself. It was in his nature to keep his emotions under wraps.

Well maybe if she hadn't been smoking and drinking so much during her pregnancy, this could have been avoided, Scott Kelly thought to himself. He too felt bad about the child. He was very fond of Jamie but he couldn't understand why she was making matters so difficult.

"I can't figure it out," Scott managed to say.

"Make that one more thing we don't understand. We have to focus on what's in front of us," Kelly said trying not to think any more about his wife's indiscretions. "We have to start concentrating on next year's campaign."

Chapter 28

Beloved but Alone

After a morning of meetings and an interminable luncheon, President Kelly dragged his weary body into the Lincoln bedroom. The challenges of his office had prevented him from taking an afternoon nap for a long time. Sorrow from his infant son's recent death pushed him down like a struggling plane unable to gain lift. Closing the door behind him he slowly removed his shoes and made his way to the window. Looking out he could see dark, ominous clouds hanging over D.C., and for the first time that day he discerned its dreariness.

He laid down atop the blue coverlet and tried to let go of the tension that gripped his neck and back. He quickly entered the state between consciousness and sleep. Thoughts mixed with memories, and he soon drifted off into a deep dream.

In his dream, his older brother William, who had died in a plane crash in World War II, appeared. Then his sister, who also died prematurely, and finally his infant son who had just passed each appeared. He reached out for them, but they disappeared in vapor. Next a warm smiling gentleman came into view. He knew it was the President of the United States, but he didn't recognize the man. He stood framed by

Assassination Point Blank

an enormous flag before a cheering crowd. But just as quickly as it came, the crowd disappeared, fading out like a scene in a movie. The leader sat alone, crestfallen, in darkness. He called out but no one answered: there was no one he could trust.

He lay motionless for a few seconds, like a boxer sprawled on the canvas. The feeling of defeat was overwhelming.

He felt the presence of someone. When he opened his eyes he saw his brother Scott, hesitating at the door.

"You must be pretty tired. Ellen said she called up here but nobody answered so I volunteered to search for you," he said smiling. "From the hallway I could hear you talking so I thought you were already awake. The agents didn't want to disturb you."

"I was dreaming," the President answered, embarrassed.

"It must have been some dream."

"Yeah, I guess it was," he answered checking his watch. He hoped his brother wouldn't ask him about the dream's depressing details. The last thing he wanted was to talk about his depression.

"You all right?" Scott asked studying his brother's face. He could sense melancholy. He could tell his brother hadn't fully recovered from the death of his infant son two months earlier. "This isn't like you. Jamie is usually the reason you run late."

"I'm fine, just a little groggy," he said, trying to shake it off. The vividness of the disturbing dream would make it difficult to forget. "I need to take a shower; tell Ellen I'll be down in a few minutes," he said, and lurched toward the washroom before Scott could press any further.

Chapter 29

Shall I Tell the President?

"Give me a few moments. I need to gather some paperwork together and we'll be ready to leave," the slender attractive woman politely informed a Secret Service guard assigned to her.

"Whenever you're ready Ms. Myers, no need to rush," the man replied, standing at attention. President Kelly regarded the man as one of his most loyal and reliable agents. He also served as a driver for the president. As a result, Kelly assigned him to look after Annie Myers.

Annie Myers's ex-husband was a major player in the CIA and her anti-war sentiments made her a person of interest for Harvey Hampton's men. Her willingness to deliver top secret CIA information to President Kelly was courageous and put her life in grave danger. It was a heroic effort to reveal some of the hidden opposition surrounding Kelly and was made more complex and risky because she was already being closely monitored.

"I have everything," she motioned as she stuffed some files and paperwork into a briefcase. "We can leave now."

"Okay, I'll bring the car around," he replied.

Moments later the agent pulled up in an unassuming automobile. After Annie Myers jumped in and shut the door behind her, he steered from the curb, checking the rearview mirror regularly to make sure they were not being tailed. He took side streets through DC. As they approached their destination he went around a nearby block once to check if any cars behind him made the same consecutive right hand turns in a row. Confident all was clear, he coasted into a nearby parking space about a block away from their destination. Annie Myers, wearing sunglasses and a scarf, exited the car curbside and proceeded at a brisk pace along the sidewalk in front and to the right of the car, staying in full view of her driver.

The address was an apartment set aside for just this type of rendezvous. She walked to the building, glancing over her shoulder along the way before arriving at a side door which she quickly entered. After making her way up several flights of stairs she knocked lightly on the suite door. It opened; behind it stood a handsome, slender middle-aged man.

"You made it. Thank you."

"It's a patriotic obligation Mr. President."

As she entered the room she removed her scarf, revealing dark blonde hair pinned up in back. Wearing a dark business suit and carrying the briefcase, she looked like an attractive attorney.

"Well this should be interesting," Kelly said, with no expression on his face. "I already have some idea of who will be on this list," he said thinking about certain journalists who betrayed him over the years.

"It was so important I could not entrust anyone else with this material," she said as she opened her briefcase and removed a folder. "Here's a partial list I was able to obtain," she handed it to the President.

"I owe you. You took proper precautions?" the President asked as he began to examine the papers. It contained the names of journalists and other members of the media who were CIA assets, individuals put into place under the CIA's Operation Mockingbird. The operation was a major infiltration and subversion of the press by the CIA with the purpose of manipulating stories and getting information for the agency's benefit. Annie's ex-husband was a founder and former head of Mockingbird. The agency had legions of agents in the press, some even watching each other.

"Yes, we were very careful, Mr. President."

She was an intelligent lady, and observant too, but one could never be too cautious. The two had known each other for many years and had been seen together in the past, but the sensitive paperwork Annie brought on this day could get her killed.

"This list is voluminous," Kelly said, shaking his head. The depth of the infestation was astonishing, even to him. But events were at least starting to make sense. He scanned the list. He noticed the name of the journalist who introduced him to his wife.

Assassination Point Blank

"Did this one catch your eye?" he asked Annie pointing to the man's name.

"Yes, it did." She could see him thinking hard, pondering the names on the list, trying to connect them back to various newspaper stories they had written. She figured he would go back and review their work. Secrecy and deceit in the media were undermining America for the benefit of a few nefarious men hiding in the shadows. Kelly had even given a speech warning Americans and urging the industry to reform. Now, he could see the juggernaut he was up against.

Chapter 30

Green will be your driver, not Streeter

It was a mid-October day and Secret Service agent Steven Streeter was patrolling the grounds of Camp David as part of his detail awaiting President Kelly's return. Although he was in good shape, only 51 years old, and had recently passed the stringent physical examination given to all the agents, he felt strange. As he walked the property an odd ringing noise began in his ear. Not thinking much of it at first, he became more concerned when a dull ache and numbness suddenly overcame his left arm.

Just a few minutes earlier, Streeter had eaten lunch with his colleagues and his stomach felt unusual. It now dawned on him to think the unthinkable; was the food he ate tainted in some way? But before he could give it further thought his chest tightened as if a 300 pound man was standing on him. He called over the radio to summon his fellow agents for help. There was no reply. *That's strange,* he thought. *Never before had they failed to stay in communication with me.*

A sudden dizziness overcame Streeter and he stumbled around in a desperate effort to reorient himself in the direction of the nearest building. It was to no avail. He staggered sideways, tripping over his own feet and crashing to the ground. Overwhelming pain gripped his chest. He flopped around on the ground like a fish pulled out of water onto the shore. He managed to cry out again for help, but only dead air and static replied.

Chapter 31

Back in the USA

On Monday morning October 21, Lew Ohlman entered the red block-shaped building facing the plaza in downtown Dallas. The property had recently been purchased by a close friend of Vice President Lionel Jones. The seven story structure was now the location of Lew's new cover job. He had started work the previous Wednesday. Once again the work was drab, this time he was positioned as an inventory clerk handling school books at the book depository. As he checked his inventory list on his clipboard, he reminded himself that cover jobs were not meant to be exciting. He looked forward to the end of the day. He hadn't talked with Julie since he started his new job and it was his turn to call. After work he would use a payphone in a discreet location he already selected to make such calls.

His weekend was eventful. Friday was his 24th birthday and Sunday his wife gave birth to a baby daughter. Sadly, all of it was overshadowed by the intrigue surrounding his espionage work. He thought about the failed mission to Mexico, after which he had been summoned back to the United States. As instructed, he smuggled the bioweapon all the way to Mexico City where he was supposed to meet a medical technician at a predetermined location in order to pass off the deadly cells. He waited, even staying multiple days in his effort to make the delivery, but his contact was nowhere to be found. He tried to get in touch with his handler, "Mr. B", but he was away in Washington, DC. Not wanting the operation to fail, Lew attempted to gain entry into Cuba on his own by visiting the consulate, but his transit visa request was denied.

Eventually, his handlers ordered him to abort and called him back to the United States. Abandon the bioweapon, it is time to return, they said. But *why would such an important mission be called off so abruptly?* They claimed the operation could not be carried out because a hurricane had wreaked havoc on the island and their contacts there and in Mexico City were in disarray. The problem with their story was that the hurricane did not hit the island until nine days later, making their explanation dubious at best. Lew kept silent. He knew they were lying.

For the time being he resided in a Dallas boarding house about three miles from his work. Meanwhile, his wife and children were placed in Irving, Texas with "friends" with ties to the intelligence community. He visited on weekends. It was for the best anyway; he loved his family, but he and his wife Martina no longer got along.

Upon relocation to Dallas his reaction was one of ambivalence. On one hand he felt relief that the risky assignment was over, but at the same time he was disappointed with its failure

Assassination Point Blank

and the uncertainty surrounding its real purpose. Something more ominous was brewing. Consumed by anxiety, he surmised that his initial suspicions were correct; the weapon had another purpose. He now doubted it was created solely to kill Fidel Castro. Castro was not the only enemy of the CIA, he contemplated. His superiors were keeping him in the dark, but why? He had a premonition they were preparing to set him up. Even if that was what they were up to, it was imperative for him to keep his cool. If he gave the slightest inkling of his suspicions, that would be it. Despite their refined looks and demeanor, they were ruthless killers. Like junkyard dogs, one false move and they'd take him out.

One evening, not long after he arrived in Dallas, they gave him a peek behind the curtain. He was approached by a handler, and brought to a meeting of powerful men. They made it known what he had suspected all along, that they represented a group intending to assassinate President Kelly. He was invited to participate in the plot. He was in a den of vipers. Questions raced through his mind. He wondered what he could do and if he could somehow thwart the plot. Could he warn President Kelly or the Secret Service? Was he himself in danger? Were they setting him up? Was there anyone on his side? Who could he trust? Should he flee the city? And if he did, would they come after him or his family? And who would be left to foil the assassination if he bugged out?

He was being watched closely, that much he knew. These were powerful and dangerous men; men who had arranged the overthrow and assassinations of heads of state around the world. It would be nothing for them to kill him if he refused to participate. He had to play along and make them believe he was in with them, even if they were setting him up. It was the only way he could get information and be in a position to stop them.

***

"Are you ok?" Julie asked over the long distance phone line.

"Yes, but I have to be careful and follow instructions if I am to get any information," he replied. He had taken precautions but he was still always nervous talking on the phone, even though it was a pay phone. He and Julie had arranged a coded method of telecommunication which was a three way call wheel that included their friend Dan in New Orleans. They both participated in the bio lab in New Orleans and were two of the only people Lew felt he could trust.

"I'm scared Lew," her voice shook with fear.

"I am too but I have to try. I still have some ideas," he said, hoping to reassure her. He went to the UN protest in Dallas where the UN ambassador was accosted by the crowd. He hated to see it happen, but maybe it was a good thing. It was covered in major newspapers throughout the country. "Maybe that will bring added security for the President when he comes to Texas," he thought as he looked out of the phone booth across the street. The pavement was wet. A light rain continued to fall and the air was still. The sidewalk nearby was desolate.

"I wish you could leave," she started to sob, holding her hand over the mouthpiece so he wouldn't hear. *He's under enough pressure*, she thought.

"I sent a warning to the FBI in Chicago," he went on. "I believe that helped. They took it serious." He was being vague on the phone but she understood. As a consequence the President canceled his trip to Chicago. Dr. Sheridan, their superior in the New Orleans lab who was also loyal to the President, gave Lew the names of trusted FBI men in Chicago. Dr. Sheridan also feared a nefarious conspiracy against the President. The failure of Ohlman's bioweapon mission heightened her mistrust. Through his participation in the Texas group, Lew discovered details of a plot scheduled for early November to kill the President in Chicago. If what he learned was true, the plan was to ambush the Presidential limo on the Northwest Expressway at the Jackson street exit. It was a ramp with a sharp 90 degree turn which would cause the car to slow to a near crawl.

"I read in the newspapers that he was sick and had to cancel his trip," Julie replied.

There was a long pause.

"These men plan on trying again soon. This time here in Dallas."

"Oh no," she gasped.

Assassination Point Blank

He wasn't sure of the location. Either at the airport, near the plaza, or at the Trade-Mart. Fortunately there were still a few people sympathetic to the President. Lew went on to explain to her that he was told there would be "an abort team" of loyal men setup to protect the President. But the details were sketchy. It did little to alleviate her fear.

"I'm worried Lew. And I miss you," she continued, wondering if she would ever see him again.

"That's all I can tell you right now. I love you," he said, cutting her off before they both broke down. There was nothing more to say.

"I love you too, Lew." The phone went dead.

Exhausted and ready to get back home, he looked around. Not a soul could be seen in either direction. He exited the phone booth in the direction of the nearest bus stop.

***

As he lay in his bed that night, Lew thought for a few moments about the man who had become his closest friend, the mercurial Jeff Morganson. They met the previous summer in Fort Worth. Jeff was originally from the Soviet Union and had become a petroleum engineer and a CIA operative as well as one of Lew's handlers, but he had since moved to Haiti in June to begin work on a special project for Arion Ostratos and some Texas oil tycoons, including Charles Merchant. Their purpose was to undertake a major development and resource exploration project on the island.

Jeff was well educated. He spoke Russian with Lew's wife and shared his experiences with Lew. They had long, intellectual conversations. He opened up and shared a lot with Jeff, perhaps too much. He now wondered how much of his personal beliefs Jeff might have passed on to others. He thought about the time he told Morganson that he was for ending segregation. Now, thinking about all the connections, he wondered how much of his views had reached the ears of the conservative Texans and CIA men conspiring against President Kelly. He tried to shake off those thoughts.

"You need to get back to nature," he could hear Jeff's voice telling him a year earlier, when Morganson and his wife returned from Mexico and Central America. It was enjoyable to listen to his friends' adventures, like hiking through the jungles in Central America. Lew yearned to abandon everything and leave for a simpler life in a foreign country with Julie.

Thoughts rushed through his head. He liked Morganson and hoped he could trust him, but he found the chameleon nature of the man worrisome. Looking back, it now made him anxious to think that Jeff could one day be conversing with him about the virtues of ending segregation and the next he would be feeling equally comfortable rubbing elbows with conservative Texas oil men. *But that was the ambivalent paradox of espionage - the simultaneous feeling of trust and paranoia,* Lew thought, reminding himself. Only now the stakes were higher. This was not a clear cut assignment. He was in the middle of a treasonous *coup d'état* plot!

He wondered exactly where Morganson fit in. Because he was one of his handlers, he left some money saved up for his family with Jeff in case anything ever happened to him on his dangerous missions. Jeff seemed to understand Lew's marital problems. He was on his fourth marriage himself. But after all that had transpired in New Orleans and Mexico, and now Dallas and the overt threats to the President, he was unsure who was on his side. Was Morganson a fellow patriot or another traitor?

* * *

"You sure he made the call to Chicago?" Angler's face stared hard through black rimmed glasses, expressionless as he inquired about an anonymous phone call received by the FBI office in Chicago. It warned about a potential assassination attempt on President Kelly in early November. Angler had gotten word.

"Yes, I'm sure." replied Mr. B. "That's why we gave him that information. It was a test and the lad failed," he continued. "He's the only one who could have that information. Now we know for sure. He's loyal to the President. But don't worry; we've made him think there are men like him inside our group, so he'll stay in position. He actually thinks he will be part of a second team setup to prevent the assassination in Dallas." The two men mirrored heartless grins.

"An abort team, huh? Good move. I suppose his views don't matter. He's expendable. In either case, we're going to use him. You handled it well. Now we know exactly how he's thinking. It was what we suspected and your idea will keep him in the right position when the time comes. That's what's important."

"He'll be there. He's wary, but either way we've got it covered," Mr. B assured Angler.

Chapter 32

What Time is it? Willy's Nightmare

Willy Eastman could still remember the incident like it was yesterday. It was in the middle of the night when he was jarred awake by the loud ringing phone on his nightstand. Groggy, he rolled his rotund, half-naked body over to pick up the receiver.

"Where in the hell is that cash?" growled an angry voice in a Southern accent on the other end of the line. Even though it was 3 in the morning Willy recognized the caller immediately. It was Lionel Jones. Willy had promised him $500,000 in campaign contribution money but was slow to deliver.

"Lionel? Lionel, is that you? What the — why are you calling me at such an ungodly hour? Do you know what time it is?"

"I didn't call you to ask you the time! I'm calling to find out where the hell that cash is. I'm sick of waiting. I want you to get to the fucking airport and bring that goddamn cash now! You hear me?" Willy knew that Lionel meant business. He reached for his glasses and wasted no time. Very shortly Lionel had his money. Willy had it all along. He was one of the richest men in Texas.

***

Years had passed since that early morning phone call. Over time Willy had partnered up

Assassination Point Blank

neck deep in business deals with Jones, using Jones's political influence to secure lucrative agriculture and energy contracts and shares of government agriculture allotments. The two business partners got some temporary relief the old fashioned way in 1961 with Harry Miller's convenient and unexpected death.

Unfortunately for Willy, it was a scandal that continued to resurface as he was brought in front of a grand jury the following year for questioning. Lionel referred Willy to a lawyer who had helped him in the past. Willy wisely took the fifth and Miller's death was ruled a suicide by the grand jury. He figured Lionel must have fixed the outcome. However, even after the grand jury decided the death was a suicide, the ordeal continued. By this time the Kelly brothers and their allies had become interested in Miller's mysterious death. They were determined to get to the bottom of the matter. *Down in Texas, Lionel Jones could have Harry Miller bumped off and could even rig a grand jury, but he didn't have absolute control in Washington and certainly not when it came to the Kelly brothers. What an endless nightmare!* Willy bemoaned. He knew this was still a big problem, even for Lionel. Willy would soon find out that Lionel had another solution.

Chapter 33

Star Light, Star Bright Nov 13, '63

By mid-November the President's staff had scheduled his Florida and Texas trips for later that month. They were two important states for electoral votes. As Governor Conway had pointed out, Texas had bitter disputes in the party which needed to be healed. President Kelly agreed to go and in the meantime he continued with his daily responsibilities while those around him made arrangements for his travel.

It was a chilly afternoon in Washington, at the time of the year when the days are short and darkness has momentum. The guests arrived on the south lawn to attend a performance of The Black Watch, also known as the Royal Highland Regiment. The group consisted of unique Scottish infantry battalions of the British Army. From the balcony, President Kelly, his wife, and the children listened to the drums and bagpipes as male soldiers in kilts marched about the lawn.

That night after the performance Miss Smith brought the children to the oval office because they wanted to spend more time with their father before going to bed. They played on the floor with the President. After some time inside, Ellen Lakeland followed Miss Smith and the children out on the steps leading to the garden. It was twilight and getting dark. James Jr. was running about chasing the pet dog when Cathy looked up into the eastern sky and pointed.

"Star light, star bright," she began.

At that moment the President came up behind them, standing silent, gazing at the sky as well.

"Star light, star bright," she repeated, still focused on the glowing heavenly body. "First star I see tonight."

"Up above the world so high," the President said and Cathy repeated.

He turned to his daughter. "Why don't you go and say that to Mommy?" He said pointing at her mother as he slowly turned to go back inside.

The planet or star in the sky that night appeared surreal to Ellen. For some reason it was frightening and mysterious. It made no sense, but a creepy feeling overcame her. Even after she went back inside, the feeling persisted. She tried to shake it off, but couldn't. Something about it haunted her.

Chapter 34

November 21, San Antonio, Houston & Fort Worth

"We've been divided in this country along so many lines. The divisiveness is holding us back from achieving our potential and true destiny," President Kelly proclaimed, gesturing with one hand as he spoke in front of a dinner party at the Coliseum. He could really deliver a speech. The Houston crowd cheered his eloquent and emotional oratory. He continued, "Just to name a few: there are the divisions in ideology, race, gender, and economic class. I believe it is the Democratic Party's destiny to be the constructive leaders in the mending of dissention in America. But we first have to start by coming together within our own party. That's the purpose for my visit to Texas, to bring the Democratic Party together!" He exclaimed enthusiastically. "Today we want to honor Congressman Tompkins. He deserves recognition. It is my hope he will decide to run for office again. For over twenty-five years his record has served its constituents and the entire country. His commitment to progress and growth has been exemplary." Kelly's speech went on to praise the longtime Congressman. He concluded his speech by saying, "In closing, with a unified Texas, the Democratic Party will continue to lead America into the last part of the 1960s."

Assassination Point Blank

During the President's speech, Lionel Jones stared at the side of Kelly's head with boiling hatred. *You're too dumb to realize Tompkins is one of us! Soon I'll be in the White House, and our people in the media will dirty your legacy with scandalous rumors. I'll show you.*

***

On his flight from Houston to Fort Worth that evening, Kelly pondered the state of his political party. In spite of his marvelous rhetoric that evening, he knew the unfortunate reality was that the Democratic Party, like other organizations he encountered as President, also had to be cleansed of corruption. He would start with his Vice President. He was determined to jettison Lionel from the 1964 Presidential election ticket once he was ready to start campaigning in earnest. In the meantime, a pragmatic understanding that Texas was vital territory had made it necessary to visit the state. So for now, here he was in Texas, in preseason campaign mode. Regrettably, campaigning with Lionel Jones brought up bad memories and created unwanted drama.

He could remember the time in 1960 when he and Lionel were on the campaign trail the first time. As they were waving to a gathering crowd a member of the audience began heckling Lionel, shouting something about the crooked vote counting scandal that helped get him elected into the Senate in 1948. When Lionel heard the man he reacted like a rabid dog. Going absolutely crazy, he whirled his large body around trying to locate the man in the crowd.

Assassination Point Blank

When he finally spotted him he shook his fist and with his powerful voice bellowed back, "You son of a bitch. Come up here you little chicken shit. I'll kill you." But the man was too far back in the crowd. James Kelly found both men's behavior reprehensible and tried to restrain Jones but it was no use. Jones knocked Kelly's restraining hands off and continued his tirade. He screamed and shook his fist at the man, "You can't get away you little bastard! I'll put the fucking evil eye on you!" James Kelly could do nothing but roll his eyes in disgust.

Unfortunately it wasn't the only such incident. Even if Lionel's temper was his only flaw, Kelly didn't want to go through it again. The scandals surrounding his Vice President which had come to the surface were gargantuan, almost beyond belief. There were even rumors that Lionel's own sister, Josephine, was murdered two years earlier because she talked about Lionel's business too frequently.

At the same time Texas was important and there were men in the state, such as Congressman Tompkins, whom Kelly felt deserved recognition and whose support he needed, especially if he was going to move forward without Jones.

Chapter 35

Late Night Ambitions, November 21-22

Kelly woke up startled. His brain was replaying the previous day's events. It took him a moment to realize the time and date and his location. He had spent the day in San Antonio and Houston with his campaign team. They flew into Fort Worth late and by now it was the early morning of November 22. Exhausted, he had fallen asleep in a lounge chair in his hotel suite. He hadn't made it to bed yet. Jamie was in another suite. He glanced at his watch; it was 1:45 in the morning. Half asleep, he moved over to the bed and turned off the lamp. He would be in for another busy day tomorrow with Lionel and the Texans.

***

It was nearly 2:00 a.m. Maggie Braun patiently waited in a room off the main foyer. She was in Charles Merchant's North Dallas mansion attending a celebration honoring FBI director Harvey Hampton. When Lionel Jones had arrived about a half hour earlier he looked drawn and seemed antsy. She didn't think he would even make it to the party. He spotted her immediately, making his way over to say a quick hello, but explained that he couldn't visit long because the men had business to discuss. No sooner than he had explained the situation a group of men led by Charles Merchant and Harvey Hampton came over and gathered around him.

"Good evening Lionel, it looks like it's been a long day, huh?" Merchant remarked.

"It sure has, Charles." Lionel nodded as he shook Merchant's hand. "We didn't arrive from Houston until late and it took me some time to be excused from my Vice Presidential duties. Sorry I'm so late," he said, scanning the group. "Good evening, Harvey. Good evening folks," Lionel continued, acknowledging all the men congregating around him.

"Okay, now everyone's here and we're ready to get started." Wasting no time, the host took the lead and motioned for the men to follow. He moved the group to a large conference room on the opposite side of the entrance hall where they could conduct their business behind closed doors. It was already set up for the twenty-six attendees.

Maggie now realized that a certain number of men at the party had been waiting the entire time for the arrival of the Vice President. She didn't know the topic of discussion but her street smarts sensed a tension in the air. As Lionel Jones's mistress and a native to the area, she was acquainted with most of the guests. In fact, Maggie's two older sisters and her brother were all married to cousins of Governor Conway, who was also at the party that evening. The Governor followed Lionel and the group of men into the private chamber.

It was late but Maggie still held out hope she could rendezvous with Lionel. While she waited, she wondered about the purpose of the late night conference. Whatever its reason, obviously it was time sensitive and certainly not trivial. Some of the most powerful men in Texas and America were behind the closed doors. She identified most, if not all the men following Merchant. In addition to Jones and Conway, there was Harvey Hampton and his constant companion, CC Tillson, the number two man in the FBI. She also recognized several prominent Texas businessmen, such as Willy Eastman and oil tycoon H.M. Hart, who was said to be the richest oil man in the country, even bigger than Merchant. And of course, Lionel's most trusted men, Clint Carson and Mo Walters, were also present.

Dick Newman, the sales manager for an Austin radio station, came wandering by from the restroom. He was one of at least a dozen members of the media at the party, many of whom Maggie knew because of her position with a Dallas advertising agency. He stepped into the doorway. His voice interrupted her train of thought.

"Hello, Maggie"

"Oh, good evening Mr. Newman"

"I almost walked right by you. It's a fine party isn't it? Mr. Merchant sure has a nice place, huh?"

"Yes, it's beautiful."

"I guess it looks like the big shots took their discussion behind closed doors," he said making conversation. "How are things going at the agency?" he asked. His station was owned by Lionel's wife, Raven.

"Very well, thanks. I notice there are a lot of important people from the media here to cover the celebration."

"Indeed, owners from the Dallas and Fort Worth newspapers, and even reps from the AP and UPI," Dick answered, eyeing the double doors where Merchant had taken the men.

"Yes, I recognized some of them."

"Well Maggie, please excuse me but I'm going back to join the party. It was nice seeing you," he said as he exited the room.

Sometime later the discussion across the hall adjourned and the men began making their way out of the conference room. The entire time Maggie had been waiting at the same table on the other side of the entrance hall. Lionel was the first to leave and came over to see her. Standing beside her chair he looked more refreshed but had a stern look in his eye. He put both hands on her shoulders and leaned over. His mouth was next to her ear. She expected him to tell her the room number of the hotel where they could meet. Instead, out of the corner of her eye she caught the serious look on his face as he said in a low, menacing voice. "After tomorrow, that son of a bitch Kelly will never embarrass me again. That's no threat, that's a promise," he growled. Maggie wasn't sure exactly what he meant, but it frightened her. She knew him well enough not to ask questions when he was in such a mood.

Assassination Point Blank

Not wasting time, he said softly "Darling, I'm sorry but some more things have come up, we're going to go out for a few drinks before we head back to the hotel. Hopefully I'll see you tomorrow, if there's time. I'll arrange for a driver to take you home."

"Okay Lionel"

Maggie didn't need further explanation, it was obvious there were important people in town that evening and evidently Lionel still had unfinished business. She remained at the table facing the foyer where she could observe the men exiting the conference room. It was late and people were finally leaving the mansion. She saw the current and former mayors of Dallas and several law enforcement officials, including the Dallas County sheriff and a U.S. marshal. Maggie recognized the lawmen from skeet shooting at the range, one of her hobbies. Politics and the shady underworld were bedfellows in Texas so she wasn't terribly surprised when she spotted Jake Rubin, the flamboyant owner of a Dallas nightclub along with two middle aged men. Merchant was bidding his guests good night and showing them out. About five or six other Texas businessmen left with the two mayors. One owned a well-known construction and oil services company.

After the crowd thinned out, two prominent men remained with Mr. Merchant in the hallway. The first one was easily recognizable; he was the presidential candidate on the Republican ticket who lost in 1960 to James Kelly. Prior to that, he was the former Vice President of the United States for eight years under the previous administration. The other man was a distinguished bald headed fellow in his late sixties. Maggie had seen him before but could not place a name with the face. Months later she would remember that he was in fact JJ McClare, the chairman of the CFR and former head of the World Bank. Tonight Maggie did not realize the full significance of the gathering. By the next afternoon she would begin to understand.

***

"Where to, Mr. Vice President?" asked the driver.

"To Fort Worth, we're going to Underground Cellars," Lionel snapped.

"Yes sir." Wasting no time the driver pulled the car down the long driveway. The lights from Merchant's mansion slowly faded out in the rear window. Part one was complete, but Lionel's evening was far from over. He was now headed to an after-hours nightclub where he would hold a private meeting with nine secret service agents. They would talk and celebrate until 4 a.m.

***

That same evening, Willy Eastman pondered the secret meeting as he traveled home in the Texas darkness. He felt a sense of relief that after the next day he would no longer be bothered by investigators, but he was still curious about the way the plot would be carried out. There was no discussion about how the murder would be executed or who would participate. The eleventh hour meeting was only concerned with the aftermath, specifically the cover-up and the handling of the evidence. Although details of the operation were sketchy, it was inferred that there would be several pairs of shooters scattered about the plaza. Most likely they would be stationed in nearby buildings. When the snipers received the signal to shoot, they would all take action simultaneously. It would be over within seconds.

Harvey Hampton reassured the men that all evidence would point to the patsy and would have to go through the FBI, which he and CC Tillson ran with iron fists. The mayor had changed the parade route and it was okayed by the Governor. The Sheriff and Dallas Police Chief were also onboard, as was the secret service. For many it would be inaction that was most needed. It was easy, most involved didn't need to know much, they merely had to play their little role, look the other way and blame everything on the young fall guy.

Yet something still nagged at Willy. He couldn't understand why Governor Conway wasn't more concerned about being a sitting duck in the limo next to the President. *For heaven's sake, by the looks of things the plaza was going to be a shooting gallery. You'd think the man would be a little nervous,* thought Willy. But Conway sure didn't show it if he was. It didn't make sense. With all the untraceable poisons and sophisticated weapons at their disposal, they could get rid of Kelly anywhere, anytime. One would think there would be less risky ways to kill the man than out on the street in broad daylight. *Maybe they just wanted to show their power and that they could do it - shock and awe - and to make an example of the young recalcitrant President.* He pondered. It made no difference though, it wasn't his problem and he didn't need to know the specifics of how the mission would be completed. The important thing was that everything was under control. *After tomorrow I'll be in the clear,* he thought.

Chapter 36

On the 33rd parallel

Lew Ohlman slept the previous night at the Pryors' home in Irving, Texas, where his wife and daughter were living. The Pryors had introduced Lew to a young man named Buhler Ferguson who lived in their neighborhood and coincidentally also worked in the TSBD building. Buhler said he would be delighted to give Lew a ride whenever he stayed at the Pryor home. The weather was overcast and it was sprinkling slightly on the way to work.

"This is for you," Ohlman said as he handed Ferguson some gas money. Something seemed odd. Buhler was especially quiet on the way to work that Friday but since Lew wasn't much of a talker he didn't mind. He watched the traffic and scenery. Before long they turned into the parking lot. It was a short distance from their employer and they normally walked together.

"Go on ahead," Buhler told Lew when he saw him standing near the car after getting out. "It's going to take me a few minutes. I need to charge the car battery."

"Do you need some help?" Ohlman asked.

"No, no. You go ahead." For some reason Ferguson was waiting for Lew to leave before he would open the trunk. *What was the big secret?* Lew thought. *Is there something in the trunk he doesn't want me to see?*

Assassination Point Blank

"Okay. Well, thanks again for the ride." He couldn't understand why Ferguson would need to charge the car battery. Most likely it was an excuse for him to be alone. The half hour drive to work should have been sufficient for the alternator to fully charge the battery. Mystified, Ohlman walked away. With President Kelly due to arrive in town that day, he was nervous enough, Ferguson's odd behavior notwithstanding.

Chapter 37

Hillman's Burden

Cliff Hillman woke early on the morning of November 22, 1963. Stress was beginning to wear on him and he hadn't slept much the night before. He went to bed late, and then spent the entire night in bed contemplating the monumental task waiting for him that day. Still deep in thought, he dragged his weary body to the shower.

Despite a drinking problem, which he kept hidden, he was one of the savviest Secret Service members of the White House detail. He had worked hard to achieve his current position in the agency. Early on as an orphan he received his education on how to survive. While others in the Secret Service made their opinions and intentions known, Hillman guarded his thoughts and personal business. Some agents openly expressed their racist attitude toward blacks and their disdain toward Catholics. But Hillman was shrewd. He was more interested in knowing what others were thinking than revealing his own views. He actually agreed with those in the agency who wanted to get rid of President Kelly.

Finally, a few months earlier, opportunity knocked. He would have an important role. There were risks in participating, but in the end it would pay off. There would be major promotions for him in the organization, and more. *That is the least they can do for me considering the risks I'm about to take,* he thought.

Chapter 38

The President's Last Speech

"Are you ready?"

"No, not yet, James," she snapped.

"Jamie, please hurry," President Kelly requested of his wife politely. "We have a breakfast speech at the Fort Worth Chamber of Commerce this morning," he reminded her. He had risen early in preparation of the busy day ahead.

"I'm almost done James. Don't rush me," she answered haughtily. He held his tongue.

This was the first time she was traveling with him domestically for campaign purposes. And up until her recent moodiness, she was well behaved and appeared to be enjoying the Texas visit. In fact, her cooperation was a pleasant surprise for the President. Nevertheless, they still slept in separate suites in the hotel the night before. At this moment she was testing his patience. His campaign team decided it would be best for everyone if they met her at breakfast. Accompanied by his campaign team and shadowed by his Secret Service bodyguards President Kelly departed. On the way over they were greeted by another enthusiastic crowd in the parking lot outside the hotel. The crowd was delighted to see President Kelly and became even more pleased when despite overcast weather and a light drizzle he still gave a brief impromptu speech.

During the short speech Vice President Lionel Jones stood on the platform behind Kelly with his hands in his coat pockets. He wore a smirk. To his right stood his most trusted right-hand man, Texas Governor, big Ron Conway. Conway looked fit for a funeral as he donned a serious expression, a long black trench coat and a boutonniere. Knowing it would be Kelly's last speech, Lionel's body language said, *you can say anything you want, you Mick bastard, but in a couple of hours you'll be dead!*

* * *

The first lady remained in her hotel room and finally appeared twenty minutes tardy. Nevertheless, her entrance was met with the loud welcoming applause of the Chamber of Commerce breakfast attendees. Audiences loved her, and this one was no exception. As James Kelly looked at his wife, for a brief moment he forgot about her private threats, aloofness, and habit of running late. Her impeccable sense of fashion and ability to become the center of the universe wherever she went made her an expensive yet valuable political asset. Like him, she could capture the admiration of audiences. It was times like this that reminded him that her glitter actually complimented his substance. After her arrival, President Kelly stood up and began his speech with a funny joke that made his wife look good and himself humble. The audience loved it.

After breakfast, they returned to their hotel room and were taken by motorcade to the Air Force base for the thirteen minute flight from Fort Worth to Dallas. Joining them on Air Force One for the short flight was Texas Governor Ron Conway and his wife Milly. They landed in Love Field at 11:38 a.m., just three minutes behind the Press Plane and Air Force Two, which was carrying Vice President Jones and Raven. The two were already waiting at the bottom of the ramp to ceremonially greet the President and first lady when they disembarked. It was here, at Love Field in Dallas, where events became especially peculiar.

Chapter 39

A Secret Service Stand Down

After stopping to greet members of the press, the flight crews, and others near the plane, President Kelly and first lady shook hands with admirers gathering near the security barriers and waved to the cheering crowd further back. As usual Kelly took extra time to acknowledge and express his appreciation for the citizenry. When they arrived at their car, Governor Conway and the first lady of Texas were already waiting.

Everyone settled in and soon the presidential motorcade began to make its way through Dallas. As the line of cars turned off Mockingbird Lane onto Lemmon Avenue, Kelly thought of the untimely death of agent Steven Streeter and wished he was still alive to drive the limousine. But he wasn't, and so Wally Green was the driver.

Next to Green, in the front passenger seat, with his unusually large square-shaped head and typical stern expression was big Troy Hellerman. Big Troy seemed to be in an even more serious mood this day, if that were possible. He was third string - the number three man in command of the White House Detail - but he was in charge of the Texas trip. It was unheard-of for the top two superiors of the

White House Detail to not make such a trip, but it was only one example of a series of oddities on this day. Behind the Secret Service men in the middle row jump seats sat Governor Ron Conway on the passenger side of the car and his wife Milly directly behind the driver. Following the same configuration, President Kelly and Jamie were situated in the rear of the limo.

As he glanced around, President Kelly briefly wondered why on this motorcade none of his Secret Service guards were stationed on the back of his limo as was their normal protocol. The sole exception was Jamie's bodyguard, Cliff Hillman, who during the route was only occasionally on the rear of the car. None of the President's men were positioned there. In fact, a few minutes earlier at the airport one of his agents, Dan Layton, was jogging alongside of the limo but for some reason he was called back by his supervisor, Everett Robinson. Robinson made a point to stand up in the Secret Service follow-up car directly behind Kelly's limousine and demonstratively call back a shrugging, bewildered Layton to the running board of the trailing car, known as halfback. As he stopped, Layton questioned Robinson's order. Out of the reach of the President's ear, Robinson angrily told Layton "Don't question me boy! I'm your boss. Stay here (at the airport) until we return! Next time you'll learn not to open your mouth!" A mystified Dan Layton remained behind.

When the President left the airport a foreboding energy like an ominous dark orb followed his car. For some reason Conway appeared uncharacteristically jittery. Kelly wondered why Conway kept turning to the outside of the car to communicate with those in the back. It seemed strange. Clearly there was something on the Governor's mind. Not giving the matter any more thought, Kelly's attention then became distracted by the noise of the crowd. Even in Texas it consisted overwhelmingly of admirers and well wishers.

Chapter 40

Amanda and Sally

On Harwood Street, about a mile or so from Dealey Plaza, stood Amanda Smith. She was able to get away from work to join her friend, Sally, to watch the Presidential motorcade. It was a slow week at the office so her boss decided it would be okay for her to take the afternoon off. An admirer of President Kelly, Amanda was excited about having the opportunity to see the procession. She knew the route because it was published in several local newspapers. The two friends met at a location a mile or so from the plaza where the crowd would not be as dense. There they hoped to get a better view. They stood around for some time waiting, when finally the motorcade came into sight.

"Here they come!" Sally exclaimed excitedly as she moved a little closer to the roadside for a better view. In the distance they could see the motorcycles and a group of large automobiles approaching. Amanda stepped forward alongside her friend.

"I hope I get a glimpse of the president. He's done so much for our country already and he's going to do a lot more," Amanda said proudly. "I'm so glad I voted for him," she continued softly almost to herself. She could tell Sally was not paying her any attention.

"I can't wait to see what the first lady is wearing," Sally said superficially.

Amanda turned to Sally. "Her clothes may be nice to look at, but I wouldn't want to pay for her outfits," she added. Amanda had always needed to work hard for her money and she considered spending on frivolous merchandise to be improper. She didn't think much of the first lady. It was hard to know for sure, but to her Jamie Kelly seemed like a high maintenance prima donna. It was President Kelly that deserved admiration, she thought.

The friends' location provided a fantastic view of the President's limousine and its occupants. President Kelly was smiling to the crowd and periodically waving. He even seemed to look Amanda directly in the eye for a split second. As usual, the First Lady stood out, this time in a flamboyant wool suite and matching pillbox hat.

"Oh, look at her pink outfit! It's marvelous. I love it!" Sally exclaimed with the enthusiasm of a schoolgirl. "She's so classy, beautiful, and impeccably dressed!" The two ladies had been friends for years but at times Sally's superficial thinking aggravated Amanda. Sally was excessively focused on fashion, status and material possessions instead of the deeper more important topics in life. She just couldn't seem to grasp higher concepts.

"Why do you care so much about Jamie Kelly? She doesn't care about you," Amanda muttered under her breath. Sally ignored her, obviously annoyed.

Amanda's remark might have been uncalled for but she couldn't help herself. In this instance she might be wrong, but most of the time she found herself to be a good judge of character and unlike the majority, she discerned the first lady to be self-centered, oblivious to the average citizen and out of touch with the American people. Jamie Kelly reminded her of the Queen of England, a high and mighty person who views others with disdain. On the other hand, President Kelly had demonstrated that he cared about the average person and had a track record to prove it. *I'm here to see President Kelly not the first lady,* she thought, keeping her tongue in check, not wanting to further upset her friend. Within a few seconds the motorcade flew past, only minutes from its final destiny at Dealey Plaza, leaving the young ladies on the curbside behind.

Chapter 41

A Snare is Set

Lew Ohlman was busy checking his note pad and filling orders. He looked at the time. It was 11:33. All day he pondered Mr. B's instructions from the night before: "Tomorrow at 11:45, before lunch, we want you to stop what you're doing and go up to the sixth floor. Go to the room in the Southeast corner of the building. Go to the corner window. That's where we want you stationed. Understand?"

"Yes, sir"

"Good. Remember 11:45"

"Yes, sir"

Lew knew the room. It was dark, dusty and filled with clutter. At that moment something hit him like a lightning bolt. Instinctively he knew not to follow Mr. B's order this time. For months suspicion and uncertainty hung in the air like the stench of death. Unsure of what to do, he had been playing it straight and following his handlers' instructions. He was in too deep. However, now he smelled danger and sensed betrayal; the impulse to abandon everything and run for the hills was stronger than ever. Damn it! He should have gotten out sooner. A fleeting fantasy about the plan to rendezvous with Julie in Mexico entered his mind. He would leave the soulless cloak-and-dagger world of espionage forever and begin anew.

Suspending the bitter past and unrealistic future, he strained to focus on the present. The patriot in him asked, what could be done right now? Intuition told him that in the sixth floor room among the boxes lurked a deadly trap. Their plan manifested in his mind. Someone was waiting for him up on the sixth floor. *All Mr. B's talk about an abort team is a lie,* he thought angrily. Sure of it, he could feel it in his gut. For the first time he fully understood how they planned to set him up. So this was it. He refused to walk into their ambush. Maybe he couldn't stop an assassination attempt, if that's what they were up to, but he could still foul up their plan. Without his cooperation everything wouldn't go down as smoothly as they thought.

He decided to throw Mr. B a curveball. Instead of heading up to the sixth floor, he went down to the first floor lunchroom known as the domino room where he sat down to eat, think, and pretend to read a section of a newspaper left on the table. Because of the pending motorcade the lunchroom was deserted except for one black gentleman sitting at a far table. Three or four employees passed through to grab their lunches, evidently on their way outside in hopes of catching a glimpse of the President.

A short time later Lew did the same and left for the front entranceway of the building. A crowd now gathered on the steps to see the procession. Lew stood inside near a large pane of glass near the side of the front entrance. He was inside but could see outside.

Employees were passing through the glass doorway to exit. It wouldn't be long before the President's motorcade would make its way through the plaza. Even now he wasn't sure how or where the President would be betrayed. He heard it could be at Love Field, Dealey plaza or the Trade Mart. Seeing where the crowd gathered and the way the police were situated it appeared the procession would come from Houston Street and make a sharp turn down Elm Street. Such an obtuse route made no sense when Main Street cut straight through the center. In such a case, if there was an ambush planned the shooting would probably begin on Houston Street, and the car would most likely be shot up before it even traveled into the plaza.

While he waited by the glass doors he thought for a moment. He was in an untenable situation. If this were a chess game, there were no good moves on the board to save the President. Time had run out. He did the right thing in not going to the sixth floor, but what about President Kelly? He tried to stay calm. Thoughts flooded his brain. He had warned the FBI about the danger in Chicago. *Was there an abort team today in Dallas? No way. It was another lie. If there was such a team I would not have been kept in the dark,* he thought.

The betrayal was dizzying. There was nothing more he could do except pray. He could only hope for the best. *The Secret Service will*

Assassination Point Blank

still be there to protect the President, won't they? He wondered. At that moment he heard someone say, "Here they come!" The lead cars and motorcycles were making the turn at Houston and Elm. For a better view, he stepped out from the entranceway onto the stairs in front of the building.

Chapter 42

Missing His Appointment with Death

On observing the first few cars in the procession make the turn at the corner of Houston and Elm Street, Ohlman's heart pounded in his chest. He braced himself. He thought he might hear gunfire when the limousine slowed at the obtuse intersection. To his surprise, the President's car made it around the sharp turn and entered the plaza without incident. Ohlman even caught a glimpse of a smiling President Kelly waving to the crowd as his car passed the front stairs of the TSBD building. As soon as it did, Lew walked back inside. He thought he might have been wrong and that maybe the engineers of the conspiracy would make an attempt on Kelly's life later that afternoon at the Trade Mart instead, or perhaps they had called off the assassination in Dallas completely.

Relieved, he obtained change for a dollar and took the stairwell near the offices up to the second floor lunchroom. On the way, he could hear some commotion coming from outside the building. He placed coins in the machine and purchased a Coke. Standing next to the machine, he started to take a sip from the bottle when a policeman burst into the room, gun drawn. Ray Trudy, the building manager stood next to the officer.

"Who are you?" the policeman demanded. Before Lew could answer, Ray Trudy spoke.

"He's alright. He works here." They could both see that Ohlman was calm and relaxed. He sure didn't look like a man running from a crime scene. "There was shooting in the plaza. The President may have been shot." Trudy said to Ohlman explaining why a gun was being pointed at him.

"Up this way," Trudy said, turning to the police officer while motioning to the stairwell. "A witness said the sixth floor. I'll show you the room." They left the lunchroom and went up the stairwell. It was the same area of the building Mr. B had ordered him to go less than an hour earlier.

Now Ohlman knew what would have happened had he followed orders and gone to the sixth floor. His premonitions about being setup were correct and materializing before his very eyes. He could almost reach out and touch the danger in the air. *Those were the two men who were supposed to find my dead body,* he thought. Luckily Ray Trudy must not have been fully apprised of the identity of the fall guy, at least not yet. But whatever was going on, it was time to get out of the building. He left through the front door. The President's car must have been ambushed seconds after he re-entered the building, Ohlman thought. They must have fired at the car as it approached the overpass toward the back of the plaza, he figured. It's not what he expected. He wondered about President Kelly.

Assassination Point Blank

Until he could contact his pilot friend Dan, who he hoped would fly him to Mexico, he had to go someplace to hide. Absent of anyone he could trust, he decided to return to the rooming house and retrieve his revolver. It would be difficult, but his desire to get out of town and leave for Mexico where he could meet up with Julie.

Chapter 43

The Sniper's Nest

The motorcade through Dallas was indeed rerouted to conveniently pass Lew Ohlman's new work place, the Texas School Book Depository Building (TSBD). Mo Walters, Lionel Jones's most trusted hatchet man, peeked out of a window on the building's sixth floor. He sat on a box just out of the sight of those below. With the help of Jake Rubin, he had setup a sniper's nest near a window in a vacant room in the Northeast corner of the floor. The two men made up one of the assassination teams stationed near the plaza. He kept a close eye on the time. It was between 12 and 12:30. Wearing a miniature radio receiver earclip, he listened for further instructions while holding a German Mauser at port arms.

Hidden in the corner of the building under some boxes near the stairway was another rifle, an Italian Carcano. *That's the piece of shit gun they will claim Ohlman used,* laughed Walters to himself. He stayed on task, focusing on the plaza and periodically glancing across the room at the doorway, puzzled as to why Ohlman hadn't appeared yet. By this time the young man's handler should have given him the directive to move up to the sixth floor. Eliminating the fall guy was actually his partner Jake Rubin's responsibility.

Assassination Point Blank

Nevertheless, it was essential for all involved.

Meanwhile, Jake stood in anxious silence, hidden in the dark shadows near the doorway, waiting to spring. He held a special CIA weapon used for incapacitation and had his .38 handy. Rubin was a stocky, powerfully built man who lifted weights regularly. He was a former boxer and despite his age had a gymnast's athleticism. He would have no trouble, especially when taking the smaller man by surprise. Besides, Mo was there if necessary. Once the mayhem started in the plaza, Rubin would shoot the incapacitated patsy and leave the building. His body and the evidence would all be handled by complicit law enforcement. That is, if the young man ever showed. The minutes ticked away and there was still no sign of Ohlman. Rubin was getting nervous. They obviously had a problem. Something had gone wrong. The motorcade was entering the plaza and their fall guy was in absentia.

From his position adjacent the window, Mo Walters watched the motorcade. As instructed, he waited to fire his distraction shots. He would not do so until after he heard a single gunshot *and* the limo passed a specified paint mark on the opposite side of Elm Street. To his surprise, the marker was at least two-thirds of the way down the plaza. Just before the car reached his marker he heard a gunshot and it was now his time to fire. Curiously, by the time he heard the first shot the limo had already made it deep into the plaza, a split second from his designated paint marker. He remained focused on his assignment. When the car reached Walter's marker, he fired his rifle toward the overpass. The rifle crack from his Mouser echoed. He heard other gunfire too, at least one of which seemed to come from the top of the Dal-Tex building behind him. His adrenaline was pumping. Watching the car as it exited the plaza, he could see President Kelly's limp body slumped across the seat. Jamie Kelly, in her bright pink outfit, was on the back of the trunk. The President's limousine disappeared under the viaduct. As it did, he detected some rising smoke from behind a picket fence off to the right hand side of Elm Street above a grassy hill. *Another member of the assassination team is over there too,* he thought. Chaos ensued. People were running in different directions. Pandemonium had overtaken the plaza.

"It's time to get out of here," he told Rubin as he set down the Mauser. Through his earpiece Mo had gotten word that the mission was accomplished. They promptly departed the sixth floor, then split up and met no resistance exiting the building. A getaway car with two CIA men was waiting for Walters. Rubin had his own transportation. For what seemed like a long time there was dead silence in the automobile as the driver calmly cruised the speed limit put distance between themselves and the plaza.

"Everything is going as planned," the driver said. Everyone in the car knew that meant the President was mortally wounded or already dead. Through the radio they likely got the word from one of the Secret Service agents in the front of Kelly's limo. Walters knew that Lionel was holding his own hand held radio that day.

"There's a problem," Walters said breaking the silence. "Rubin had to go Parkland."

"What do you mean? What kind of problem?" a man up front asked.

"For us, things didn't go exactly as planned." From the backseat Walters explained to the men what had happened.

To stay in contact with their superiors, the two CIA men also wore radio receiver earclips. After a conversation with someone on the other end, the driver turned to Walters. "We're going to Oak Cliff." It was no surprise; they were heading in that direction anyway.

The CIA official sitting in the passenger seat opened his beige jacket and double-checked his automatic pistol. He turned to Walters in the back seat and said, "I guess the day's excitement is not over yet. They say we still have more work to do," he sighed. "It looks like we've got to make a cop killer out of this guy." It must have been a contingency order. Apart from their now obvious search for Ohlman, Walters could only hear one side of the radio conversation. He wasn't sure what information had come in for the two CIA men, but he was with them if needed.

Everything transpired so quickly. Mo thought about the events in the plaza. He realized his gunfire served as a distraction so that witnesses would point to the TSBD as the location of the sniper. Everything happened so instantaneously he couldn't be sure how many shots were fired, and from how many locations, but strangely he swore the first seemed to come from the motorcade and the vicinity of the limo itself.

In preplanned timing, the police would arrive at the TSBD to secure the area and find Ohlman's dead body. The media would explain to the world that the police were forced to kill a skinny deranged Marxist assassin in a gun battle. They were prepared to plant a handgun on him in the event he was found unarmed. Ohlman would be described to the world as a lone malcontent, a nut, a wiry insane little man. The death of President Kelly would simply be written off as a meaningless random act of violence and the case would be swiftly closed. The Marxist assassin angle was well thought out. It would set up a further escalation of the cold war and a pathway to a new war in Vietnam. At least that was the plan.

But now with Ohlman missing, the entire operation was thrown into chaos and his disappearance was not the only matter puzzling Walters at the time. Being such an accurate marksman, he couldn't understand why he was instructed to merely shoot distraction rounds. He was a dead eye with a rifle from 100 yards, making it impossible to comprehend why the architects of the conspiracy didn't allow him to take the oncoming kill shot at the corner of

Houston and Elm. The limousine was traveling toward him and conveniently had to slow in front of his sniper's nest, just before it was to take the sharp left hand turn. Granted, any shot with a rifle was dangerous, especially with Lionel's friends, Governor Conway and his wife in the car. Nevertheless, surely that shot made the most sense. He was surprised that Conway and Lionel would take such a risk with rifle fire. Wasn't there a better way to take the man out?

Or could that first shot have come from in or near the car, perhaps by a Secret Service agent? He wondered. For a split second, he thought he saw gun smoke near the car. But he couldn't worry about the specifics for very long, in this operation nobody seemed to know all the answers. What difference did it make anyway? He figured Lionel and the other planners must have their reasons. Now, with Lew Ohlman missing, he had more important concerns.

Chapter 44

Dark Magic in the Occult Plaza: Six Seconds in Slow Motion

It was midday as the line of automobiles approached the plaza. The sun was at its highest point in the sky; it was the time of day when the perpetrators would do their father's work. Following the three lead automobiles and police motorcycles in front, Wally Green steadied the heavy car as it made the sharp 120 degree turn at Houston and Elm and entered the plaza. Green continued to drive at a slow rate of speed along the straightaway.

Upon entering the plaza Kelly noticed once again the lack of Secret Service guards on the back of his car and he wondered why the police motorcycles assigned to guard his car were not in their typical protective pattern. In fact, the group of motorcycles that were supposed to secure the car started to drop back behind the limousine as it made its way deeper into the plaza. The President smiled and waved to the crowd. Someone on his right side got his attention for a moment and he gazed in that direction.

About that time, Milly Conway turned to him and said "Mr. President, you can't say that Dallas doesn't love you." With her words began a torrent of events. From his blind side came a

Assassination Point Blank

sharp prick on the neck, like a needle. It stung like an insect bite and burned. An instant reaction caused his eyes to close tightly as he lost vision. Unable to see, he clinched both fists using his lower palms in an effort to rub his eyes, but it was to no avail. Then, almost instantaneously his breathing seized. Fighting for oxygen and unable to see, he tried desperately to breathe. He kept both arms up near his face but after only a second or two of struggling he began to slump forward in his seat, debilitated. Everything was turning dark, as a powerful CIA drug overtook his system. Unable to see or breathe, he could still feel his wife to his left. For some reason she was stiffly holding him away from her with gloved hands. Then, after Conway said something more to her, she pulled his left arm down. He feebly tried to hold his arm up, but it was no use. He was spiraling into darkness. In no time flat his strength ebbed. He hunched forward; still locked in position by the gloved hands.

It seemed like an eternity, but only a second or two had elapsed as the instructions went from the front of the car to the back. Big Troy Hellerman turned to Milly Conway seated diagonally to his rear and gave the signal. Troy had been scanning the north side of the street. "Ok, it's time!" He demonstratively prompted Milly and the Governor to action just before the car approached one of the yellow paint marks on the curb.

Assassination Point Blank

By this moment the President had no strength left but he could still hear Governor Conway saying something bizarre to Jamie. Whatever was said, it cued Jamie into action. At the same time as his coded command, Conway motioned to Milly with his white cowboy hat in hand. Like the flipping of a switch, all the participants in the car burst into their final coordinated act.

Governor Conway was seated on the passenger side of the limousine. As rehearsed, he awkwardly twisted his upper torso to his right into an unorthodox position. He faced the outside of the car rather than the inside as would be the conventional manner of communicating with people seated in the rear. He had his reasons; turned in such a manner his entire back faced Milly sitting next to him. From such a position he accomplished three things: First, turning his neck another ninety degrees like an owl, he could check the condition of the President and Jamie in the rear seat. Secondly, having foreknowledge of the patsy's whereabouts, he could later claim he did this because heard a shot emanating from the TSBD building. And most importantly, it was imperative for him to be turned in such a way for Milly to do her part.

While her husband's entire back was facing her, Milly Conway briefly glanced up front at Big Troy who implored her, "It's time. Let's go, now!" Using both hands she aimed the tiny canister at her husband's back and sprayed a dark red colored substance on his suit jacket.

Meanwhile, the Governor observed President Kelly hunching forward, becoming incapacitated. The drug rapidly spread its way into his system, exactly as intended. Conway locked eyes with Jamie, who despite wearing long white gloves, continued to hold her husband away, as rehearsed. Like a mind controlled zombie, her wide-set eyes hypnotically stared back at the Governor, awaiting his instructions. For a brief second, their eyes held. He knew she was firmly in her alternate state. She pulled the President close. Confident that the incapacitation agent had fully taken hold, Conway waited no longer and gave Jamie her MK-ULTRA trigger words, while he simultaneously turned back around to face the front of the car. Fully engulfed in a mesmerizing trance, she was now in character and compelled to perform her reprehensible act.

Like the Luciferian magician, from under the seat emerged the second gloved hand holding a .38 snub nose revolver. With one hand she pulled her husband close and with the other she pressed the muzzle of the gun to James Kelly's temple and pulled the trigger. For a nanosecond a yellow-orange muzzle flash from the barrel appeared in the locality of the President's head. Jamie's hand jerked back and upward into the air from the gun's recoil. The bullet entered the left side of the President's skull. It blasted out a large piece of the back rear section of his head on the opposite side. Blood, brains, and bone fragments flew into the air. For a brief moment, barely detectable, a faint trail of smoke lifted behind the left side of President Kelly's head. Immediately, Jamie was certain that one bullet was adequate. It extinguished the life of her hated spouse, the man whom her alternate personality was programmed to envy and despise. Just then as rehearsed, she yelled out "My god, he's shot!"

All of the participants in the car, being fully aware of what was to transpire, were turned completely around, for perhaps a second, rubbernecking like psychopathic spectators until the fatal headshot was delivered. They had been sitting upright the entire time; only when the loud explosion of the revolver's kill shot shook the automobile did they turn forward to duck.

Even Wally Green, the driver, was twisted around in his seat taking a gander as the President's head shattered. However Wally had another important reason for looking over his shoulder; as part of the plan, he was waiting for Cliff Hillman to arrive on the back of the car. In his mirror he could see Hillman racing to catch up.

After efficiently slaying her husband, Jamie robotically moved to her next task which was to return the snub nose revolver to its rightful owner, Cliff Hillman. In so doing, she callously flung her husband's dead body away as though it were a repulsive dead animal carcass. Next, as was rehearsed, she looked behind the car to locate Cliff, but he was off time and had not yet reached the rear of the limousine to be in position to retrieve the weapon as expected. Hillman had stumbled over the uneven pavement and nearly tripped before clumsily recovering his balance and grabbing a back handle to pull himself up on the car. His late arrival was the first blunder in what had been a sequence of flawless teamwork.

Trapped between mental states, Jamie feared that Wally Green might mistakenly floor the accelerator at any moment before Hillman could jump aboard. A sudden impulsive fit of hysteria overcame her. Leaving the revolver, she scrambled over the back seat onto the trunk in a desperate effort to find Hillman. The tardy Hillman finally made it, jumping onto the car and returning Jamie to her seat. Only when Hillman was safely on the back of the car did Wally vigorously gun the engine. The limousine tires bore down on the pavement as the car sped out of the plaza into the dark tunnel and onto the ramp leading to the freeway. The lines on the road blurred beneath the car as it picked up speed like a jet plane on a runway.

At the time when Jamie was on the back of the car, the Governor was doing his part. With the stealth of a ferret, he had swiftly snuck into the back seat and adroitly retrieved the revolver and drug delivering paraphernalia. He would later claim that he was lying unconscious from a massive bullet wound in his back and chest. The entire event took only about six seconds.

***

The follow-up car, known as Halfback, trailed immediately behind the Presidential limousine and carried ten men, eight of which were secret service agents. Stationed on Halfback's front running boards were Special Agents Cliff Hillman and Tom Riley. Normally, two agents would be riding on the back of the President's limousine directly behind the president and first lady, but on this day they were not. As part of the stand down, they had been instructed by their superiors to stay off the President's car and instead ride on the follow-up car's running boards. Hillman knew the reason, but his colleague Tom Riley was evidently absentminded or out of the loop and mistakenly followed Hillman's lead in jumping off the follow-up car. Like Hillman, around the time of the fatal shot Riley too ran ahead toward the President's car. His boss, Assistant to Special Agent in Charge, Everett Robinson, acted as he did earlier in the day with agent Dan Layton, and wasted no time calling Riley back. After taking a few steps Riley stopped running to the President's car and returned to his position on the follow-up car.

In contrast, Cliff Hillman continued on to the President's limousine. With the exception of Riley's false start, all the President's secret service agents in the plaza followed their stand down orders and did nothing. The exception was Hillman, who was to perform the first and most important step in the cover-up.

Finally, after his initial delay, Hillman caught up, grabbed the handle and steadied himself on the back of the car. He returned the First Lady to her seat, retrieved his weapon from Conway and then nervously fumbled with it while removing the spent cartridge as the limousine sped through the underpass. Hillman uncomfortably straddled over Jamie and President Kelly's dead body. So positioned, he had a bird's eye view of the gory, macabre sight beneath him; President Kelly's twisted body lay across the bloody seat, a large region of his skull was torn open and some blood was still oozing out of the disgusting head wound as the body convulsed. Blood covered the President and First Lady.

The downfall of President Kelly was carried out, although Hillman's tardiness in getting to the Presidential limousine disrupted the entire timing and smoothness of the assassination and left additional clues. First, because he was out of position, Jamie panicked and climbed onto the rear trunk. Wally Green was thus forced to slow the automobile to a suspiciously slow rate, at one point almost braking the car to a standstill while waiting for Hillman. He also had to avoid throwing the first lady off the back. It wouldn't matter. Nobody would piece it together and if they did they were powerless to do anything anyway.

***

Dealey Plaza, located on the thirty-third parallel in downtown Dallas, is architecturally a place of mysticism and powerful occult symbolism and magick. Its arcane design was created by modern practitioners of the mystery schools of ancient Babylon. It is laid out as an outdoor druid temple of the sun and divided into four quadrants or seasons. From an aerial view, one can more easily discern how the roads in and around the plaza form two dimensional geometric shapes such as triangles. These triangles could also be thought of as pyramids. The base of one is formed by Houston Street, with Elm Street and Commerce Street forming the sides. The pyramid is bisected by Main Street, the center road in the plaza, creating two additional smaller oblique pyramids. The tops of all three pyramids are truncated by the railroad overpass. Thus all three pyramids are missing their capstones and eyes. Without their capstones they might also be considered trapezoids — the ideal shape for a ritual alter. The unique street layout additionally forms the devil's pitchfork, known as the trident of Neptune-Poseidon.

Inside the plaza stands a white stone obelisk partitioned into the 14 sections of Osiris with a flame on top. It is positioned alongside one of the two reflecting pools. With layered meanings the flame represents the sun god, the light of Lucifer, Osiris, or Ra as well as the illuminated man. The obelisk points up toward the sky, while it's reflected image in a pool of water points down, conveying the symbolic axiom in the occult, *as above so below*. Near the plaza on the opposite side of the Stemmons Freeway and triple overpass flows the Trinity River.

Dealey Plaza in Dallas Texas was the ideal location for Kelly's assassination. Not only was it Jones and Conway's home turf but it also is a place immersed with evil occult power. Dallas lies along the 33rd parallel or 33rd degree of latitude. This is compelling as the highest degree in the Scottish Rite of freemasonry is the 32nd degree. The meritorious 33rd degree is only bestowed upon those who contribute meaningfully to the advancement of the plan and the culmination of the Great Work. The Great Work being the bringing in to the world of The New World Order, a one world totalitarian government ruled by the illuminated man. The number of that man is 666. The importance of the number six was unmistakable: Six shots, six shooters? The sixth floor, six seconds, six in the car.

The assassination of President Kelly was actually a public sacrifice. Their treachery did not go over as flawlessly as the collaborators had hoped; nevertheless, the elite men of the Secret Brotherhood achieved their goal. They vanquished the one man who stood in the way of their wicked plans for a New World Order. They made an example of him by executing him in public. Their brutal act traumatized the populace and created fear and sadness, which in their evil, twisted spiritual dogma gave them yet more power. Their belief was that fear and trauma drains energy from the victim, in this case a mass collective victim, the entire nation, and gives it to the perpetrators. Like vampires, the Secret Brotherhood would suck the energy out of an entire nation, assuring that the Brotherhood would stay in power for decades. As a true

American Patriot died in the backseat of the limousine, there was little now to stop their jack boot march to a New World Order!

Revelation 12:9 - *and the great dragon was cast out, that old serpent, called the Devil, and Satan, which deceiveth the whole world: he was cast out into the earth, and his angels were cast out with him.*

Part II

Chapter 45

The Cover-up Begins

The cover-up whipped into high gear even before the limousine arrived at Parkland Hospital. As the car sped down the freeway, the participants began disposing of physical evidence. Once on the Stemmons Freeway, Hillman opened the cylinder of his revolver and removed the one empty shell casing. He flung it out of the car, quickly replacing it with a new one from his pocket. At the same time the Governor and Milly took care of the drug delivery device used to incapacitate the President as well as the red spray. The idea of making the Governor a victim in such a fashion was brilliant and would surely enhance his political future. His "injuries" would also serve to divert any possible suspicion of involvement of those in the limousine. As the car roared down the freeway, Jamie remained stuck in a trance.

Six minutes later the limo made it to Parkland Hospital.

"Hurry up and get them out of the car!" someone yelled. Because he was in the jump seat blocking access to the President, the Governor was removed from the limo first. It took time. The man was a great actor; his large heavy body lay limp like a sack of potatoes as he faked unconsciousness. They wrestled his dead weight onto a stretcher and wheeled him inside, ultimately into trauma room 2 where a "life saving operation" would be conducted.

President Kelly was first seen by the junior surgery resident, Dr. Corsico, in the ER "pit" area of the hospital. In a semi-private cubicle adjacent to the pit, they quickly cut him out of his clothes and Dr. Corsico took a laryngoscope and placed an endotracheal tube into the President's trachea and connected it to a breathing machine.

Shortly thereafter Kelly was moved into trauma room 1 where Dr. Jensen was controlling an anesthetic breathing bag while two other doctors were making a transverse incision into the president's neck as they performed a tracheostomy. It was at this point when Dr. Roland McClain and Dr. Chris Cavanaugh entered the room. They could see the president was also hooked to an ECG monitor. With such a large head wound they wondered if he still had a heartbeat.

"Dr. McClain, come here and hold the retractor," one doctor requested. McClain did as instructed, holding the retractor in place to help them open a new airway.

McClain could see that all these procedures were unnecessary. For all intents and purposes, the man was already dead. Even if there was a heartbeat, there was absolutely no hope he could survive. The head wound was just too fatal.

Dr. Jensen indicated to Dr. McClain that he had earlier seen a small hole in the President's left temple, but now that his head was covered with blood and turned in the opposite direction, McClain couldn't get a good look. However, from where he stood he could easily observe through the large gaping wound on the right rear side of the skull, that most of the right back half of the President Kelly's brain, right cerebral lobe and cerebellum had been destroyed. While the tracheostomy was being performed McClain even witnessed a portion of the cerebellum oozing out of the large head wound. *They are wasting their time. There is no reason for performing this surgical procedure,* he thought. He was correct. Shortly thereafter President Kelly was pronounced dead.

A Catholic priest entered the room. He lifted the sheet off the President's head and performed last rites. Jamie Kelly had been back and forth between the trauma room and the hallway but was now in the room. When the priest was finished she removed her wedding ring and placed it on her husband's finger.

***

In another section of the hospital Lionel and his team were getting restless. He had waited 15 years and was anxious for power. Before the President's death, arrangements had already been made by the Secret Service for a coffin to be delivered and a priest to come issue last rites. A judge would have to be contacted to swear Lionel in as the next president as soon as possible.

They planned on taking Kelly's body with them on Air Force One, but they were being halted because the Dallas coroner, Ed Reece, insisted that according to state law it had to remain for autopsy. Jamie Kelly applied pressure, insisting that she would not leave without her husband's body and Lionel Jones said he wouldn't leave without Jamie Kelly, but Reece remained steadfast. Big Troy and other secret service agents were using intimidation tactics. They were desperate to take possession of the most important piece of evidence. By this point, their façade of professionalism had vanished. Reece stood up to them, but he was heavily outnumbered. He tried to block the hallway. An ugly argument ensued, threats were exchanged and ultimately Reece was physically pushed out of the way into a wall. He couldn't win. State law or not, he was forced to acquiesce. Unknowable to Reece, the killer, the murder weapon and the body would now all be in the hands of the cabal. Lew Ohlman, their fall guy, was the only wild card remaining.

Chapter 46

Rubin Visits the Hospital

Seconds after the President's limo disappeared under the triple viaduct, a bewildered and distraught Jake Rubin hurried out of the TSBD building and also rushed to Parkland Hospital. Shortly after his arrival he found the men he needed.

"He got away," Rubin muttered almost unintelligibly in the chief's ear.

"What? Is that why you're here? To tell me that?" the chief said, pulling Rubin aside. "I knew something went wrong, Jake. What the hell happened?" Jerome Curbey, the bald-headed Dallas police chief probed, trying to keep his voice down, even though with all the commotion nobody could hear their conversation anyway. Curbey's face was beet red. He already knew the "assailant" had slipped away via his police radio. Ohlman was supposed to be dead on the sixth floor by now, but he wasn't. The plan was botched. As if by clairvoyance, a description matching that of Ohlman went out over the police radio at 12:45.

"Like I said he got away," Rubin repeated.

"Yeah, I see that." The chief appeared angry but not surprised. "Stay right here and keep your mouth shut." Chief Curbey disappeared. He came back promptly with two other men. One was the Special Agent in Charge

(SAIC) of the Dallas Secret Service, Woody Sorrens, and the other was someone Rubin knew to be a CIA man.

"Let's go in here where we can talk." They pulled Rubin into a private room and closed the door. One of the chief's officers guarded the outside of the door. They didn't waste any time with Rubin.

"What happened?"

"I don't know, he never came upstairs," Rubin tried to explain.

"You realize this creates a goddamned problem for us, don't you Jake?" Curbey said condescendingly. "This whole thing should already be wrapped up. You know I don't have time to be babysitting you. The media is out there and I have to talk with them."

"It's not my fault..." Rubin tried to defend himself.

"Shut up and listen. That was your assignment and you fucked it up," The chief chastised Rubin. "Now we'll have to try and clean up your mess. The question is will we bring the boy in and when we do will he be dead or alive. But there's something more. Did you allow him to get away? Did you tip him off, Jake?"

"No. No, of course not! You know I wouldn't do that."

"You better not be lying. And you better pray to God we catch him." Rubin understood what Chief Curbey was trying to say. If Ohlman escaped there would be no quick closure to the case. Rubin would be a dead man walking for letting him get away. If they brought Ohlman in alive, it could be worse if he talked. What would they do to him? The young man knew extensive information about Rubin's illegal activities and also had the ability to reveal secrets that could start to unravel the entire plot. Rubin wished for something that would get him off the hook. *Maybe the police will kill Ohlman in a shoot out,* he hoped.

"We may still need you. You understand?" Woody Sorrens said. Rubin nodded. The whole time the CIA man had been studying Rubin with the unchanging eyes of a poker player. The chief on the other hand was being direct.

"That's right," The chief tore in again. "We're not done with you yet. I suggest you stick around your place for the next few days where we can find you." Rubin got the message loud and clear. He hoped they would be more understanding but they weren't. He was being held accountable. Forget leniency, these men weren't convinced of his story. They may have thought he tipped off Ohlman or perhaps they were just upset with the situation, he wasn't sure. But in either case it was bad news for him. He knew deep down they'd be watching. He would hear from them again soon.

"We don't have any more time. Now get out of here," the chief said as they all stood. Rubin could feel their piercing eyes on his back as he left the room.

★★★

Woody Sorrens and Chief Curbey immediately went to find Lionel Jones to keep him informed.

A doctor already issued a release to the press pronouncing President Kelly dead.

"Remember the three things that we discussed last night?" Lionel was telling, not asking. He was referring to the murder weapon, the body, and the patsy. "Well right now we've only completed one out of three. We're going to stay here until number two is handled," he said looking at Curbey. "You make sure they take care of number three. Understand?"

"Yes sir," Curbey nodded. "We're already making arrangements, Mr. President."

***

As Rubin was leaving the hospital he saw a group of doctors and nurses moving about with concerned expressions. He bumped into a journalist he knew, Sam Kaplan, and said hello.

"Isn't this terrible?" Rubin said, shaking Kaplan's hand and trying to hide his anxiety.

"It sure is," Kaplan replied noticing extreme distress on Rubin's face. He found it a little unusual for Rubin, a nightclub operator, to be at the hospital.

"I'm thinking of closing my businesses as a gesture of respect. Do you think I should?"

"I think it's a good idea. Please excuse me, Jake. I have some work to do." Kaplan moved away toward someone he wanted to interview.

Chapter 47

Lew Ohlman, the Lamb is on the Lam

After departing the confusion of the plaza, Lew found his way back to the rooming house. He entered the building and headed quickly in the direction of his room. His landlady, Darlene Roberson, spotted him from the front room where she was busy adjusting the TV set. She looked up. "Oh, you're sure in a hurry," she remarked. He didn't reply. *What in the hell am I supposed to do?* He thought. *Sit down over coffee and explain to her how the police and CIA set me up for the assassination of President Kelly and are now in the process of hunting me down?* He continued to his room, retrieved his revolver and departed on foot in the direction of the bus stop.

His narrow escape from an appointment with death on the sixth floor of the TSBD merely delayed his betrayers' plans. Like the Judas goat, whose job it is to lead the sheep to the slaughter, Mr. B, Mr. Bishop, or whatever his name, nearly led him to his grave. *The planners will still try to make a scapegoat out of me,* he thought anxiously. He figured that by now, surely CIA contract hit men and the police were searching for him. He needed to get out of town.

Days earlier, he did his best in preparing a tenuous contingency plan. He hoped that he still had a few trustworthy people willing to help. In the event he was being setup, arrangements were made to meet a messenger in the Texas Theatre about a mile or so from his residence. From that person he could get further information about where and when to meet up with his friend Dan from New Orleans or another pilot who could fly him to Mexico. There were occasions in his espionage career when one would exchange information with another operative in a theatre. It was also a public place where he hoped he would be safe. Their plans, set a few days earlier, were all on a contingency basis, but Julie promised to meet him once she got word of his whereabouts in Mexico.

Chapter 48

The Theatre

A justifiably paranoid Lew Ohlman made his way to the Texas Theatre, his initial destination before he would leave town. Once inside he started to hear sirens blaring in the distance. *Oh great, have they already put out an APB with my description as the President's killer?* He worried. Spooking him further was that on his way, not far from the theatre, the manager of a shoe store was watching him like a hawk. The man seemed to study his every move as he stood in the doorway of his store.

Although he had money in his pocket, the stress of his predicament rattled him and he absent-mindedly forgot to purchase a ticket at the counter. He made it inside nevertheless and chose a seat near the rear center. In the darkness he glanced about trying to recognize a person serving as the messenger. He didn't notice anyone. He wasn't seated long when at least a dozen or more uniformed policemen barged in to arrest him. They first shut down the movie projector and on came the lights.

"That's him," he heard a man yell from the stage. It was the shoe store manager along with an employee of the theatre. They pointed toward the back and center, directly at him. Now that the lights were on he could see all the policemen, perhaps a dozen or more. Several big officers hustled over to arrest him.

"A cop killer," angrily remarked one of the hulking officers. His eyes burned with rage.

"What?"

"Don't play dumb with us. You shot one of our men on Tenth and Patton," the big man said as he grabbed Lew's arm. He tried to pull away. A scuffle ensued, but it was no use. One lanky cop punched him on the side of the head, cutting his brow. Another put him in a headlock while a third held him down and applied handcuffs. *Did he say a policeman has been shot?* He thought. That must have been the initial sirens he heard. He couldn't figure out how they would know so quickly he was in the theatre unless someone in military intelligence or the CIA tipped them off. When they pulled him from the floor he saw at least a dozen more policemen. *For there to be that many police officers in the theatre somebody talked,* he thought.

"Sir, I didn't shoot anyone," he declared loudly in front of any potential witnesses in the theatre.

"Shut up!" The officers took his gun, searched him and then dragged him outside where there were just as many officers and a fleet of patrol cars already parked.

How incompetent the Secret Service and Dallas PD were a little earlier in the day when it came to the important job of protecting President Kelly. Suddenly, they have become adept in moving at lightning speed to set me up as the fall guy! He thought sarcastically. His premonition of being set up was coming true. A crowd was already gathering outside. Some cried out, "Kill him! Kill him!" It was like a scene before the crucifixion.

Chapter 49

Lionel Steps over the Dead Body

Congressman Alex Tompkins winked at Lionel. They were aboard Air Force One and Jones was being sworn in by a Federal Judge to become the next President of the United States. "I do solemnly swear that I will faithfully execute the Office of President of the United States, and will to the best of my ability preserve, protect, and defend the Constitution of the United States." His right arm was raised while his left hand rested on the Catholic missal that belonged to James Kelly.

Jamie Kelly, tear-faced, stood nearby in a daze. Snapped out of her alternate personality, she couldn't remember the events in the plaza. *Did I climb on the back trunk of the limousine?* She tried to think. She couldn't quite remember. Her mind seemed to be playing tricks on her. She refused to leave Dallas without her husband's body or to change out of her pink wool suit, covered with his blood. Look what "they" did to him, she justified in her mind. Technically, she was partially correct. She certainly hadn't acted alone, and wouldn't be the only individual to benefit from the death.

Raven Jones, beady-eyed and alert, also stood near. Her husband's elusive dream was finally realized. Since 1937 he had left the dead behind to ascend the political ladder in Texas. Today, with the CIA's help, he stepped over a President's dead body and became President himself, finally obtaining the power and prestige he always coveted.

Lionel refused to leave Dallas without Jamie Kelly and the body. Everything was now going his way. His team of co-conspirators managed to load James Kelly's corpse onto the plane. Even better, before departing, word had come that the patsy had been arrested in a theatre. Military intelligence had tipped off the Dallas Police. Everything was now set to begin the transformation of America and Lionel Jones was finally flying high and on top of the world! So he thought. He didn't realize it then, but the next nine years would not unfold the way he imagined. He wouldn't have autonomy. He'd be the puppet of his bosses – the central bankers and the CIA.

Mark 8:36 – *For what shall it profit a man, if he shall gain the whole world, and lose his own soul?*

Chapter 50

In Captivity

My God, is this the same country I risked my life for in the military? Lew asked himself.

During the past 48 hours, spanning three days in captivity, Ohlman had been interrogated without a stenographer or tape recorder – an unprecedented practice. With such serious charges hanging over his head he couldn't believe a tape recorder still hadn't been obtained. Dallas Police Captain Fitz was doing most of the department's dirty work, along with an FBI agent and a detective or two. At one point, a judge came to the interview room, ostensibly to aid Lew in search for legal counsel, but he proved useless.

During questioning, they showed him pictures. He studied the photos for a moment. Immediately he discerned them to be fakes. He never posed for such photos. They were so poorly fabricated that it was easy to see that his head had been superimposed onto another man's body. The person was standing in an odd position. Was it some secret society pose he wondered? The shadows in the photo's background were also inconsistent. They were clearly propaganda pieces created earlier. He was holding a rifle in one hand and communist pamphlets in the other. It wouldn't be difficult to prove they were counterfeit, he thought.

Initially they didn't tell him that he was being charged with the President's murder. He was being held for the murder of a patrolman named J.T. Tippin who had been shot and killed. *CIA hit men probably killed Tippin,* Lew thought, after learning a little more about what had happened. The shooting was in the general area of his rooming house and Tippin's death now created a stronger frame-up against him. Naturally the event stirred up a hornets' nest of indignation in the entire police department.

He knew what they were trying to do. *But why did they choose to kill Tippin in particular?* He mused. Could he have been a corrupt patrolman involved in narcotics and other dirty CIA dealings? If so, Tippin was probably in trouble for something like taking more than his share out of the till. Or perhaps it was the unlikely opposite; Tippin was an honest patrolman who got in the way or who was too honest to go along with the planners. But no matter the reason, Tippin was dead.

Lew thought about it. If they could convince everyone that he was a cop killer, then people would easily be convinced that he had to be the President's assassin. Being framed for Tippin's death, he was now staring into the abyss. It showed just how far they would go to frame him.

Reporters demanded to see him. They were allowed to do so, briefly, when he was being

Assassination Point Blank

transferred from one room to another or to jail. On one occasion he thought he might be able to get some information out but he was interrupted and not given a chance to say much. However, during one brief instant in front of the press he declared his innocence and requested legal representation.

He hadn't shot anyone, but how could anyone prove a negative – especially while locked up? At another point, while being escorted down a hallway, he managed to blurt out to reporters, "I'm just a patsy." It was the simplest way to describe the convoluted situation in one sentence, and without legal representation it was the best he could muster.

Chapter 51

Rubin's Betrayal

It was 11:15 on Sunday, less than 48 hours after the assassination of President Kelly. The world wept. A nation was in mourning and Jake Rubin was en route to place the capstone on the cover-up. He needed to finish his initial assignment. He strolled from a nearby Western Union store unimpeded into the Dallas police station's garage.

"Don't worry about getting inside," the CIA men and police told him during their little visit the night before. "Either we'll get you a press pass, or we'll make sure the officer guarding the ramp lets you through."

He was ambivalent toward his assignment from the beginning because unbeknownst to many, Rubin had actually been "friends" with Lew Ohlman for years. At times they both worked as contract employees for the CIA. He even knew Lew's uncle, a bookmaker in New Orleans, and was like an uncle himself to the young man. None of that mattered now though, this was business. He had no choice. There was no such thing as friends in the world of espionage.

On the bright side, Rubin was led to believe that his own fate was not a dead end. The big boys floated to him the possibility of a mistrial or at worst a light sentence. It was doable. He merely had to look at Mo Walters, a hit man who had gotten away with murder. Lionel and his powerful Texas friends no doubt had a hand in the Walters trial and they could do the same for him, he thought. They were giving Jake a second chance to finish his assignment. Unfortunately, in order to save himself, he needed to betray and sacrifice Lew. It was nothing personal, just business.

He might even be hailed a hero for killing "the President's assassin," he was convinced. At first glance, this wasn't a totally outlandish thought. A great number of the populace already had a mob mentality and wanted Ohlman lynched. The media gathered momentum against the young man by jumping out of the gate fast with their "official story." Strengthening the audience's subconscious mind to remember John Wilkes Booth, like a mantra they started referring to Ohlman as the President's assassin. They used his full name, Lew Hardy Ohlman. Forget about alleged assassin or innocent until proven guilty, propaganda could make a villain a hero and a hero a villain. With such dynamics, Rubin still had a way out.

***

In semidarkness, Jake stood in the parking garage near a group of reporters who were waiting for Lew Ohlman to come down the elevator and through a corridor for transfer to the county jail. Jake's wait wasn't long, for in reality the police were waiting for him. Soon the doorway opened. Ohlman appeared.

Assassination Point Blank

Fittingly, they had him dressed for his own funeral - in all black. He was escorted by two tall policemen. His right wrist was handcuffed to homicide detective Jerome Leavengood, who was purposely wearing a white suit and cowboy hat that day. It provided a perfect contrast to Ohlman's dark clothing.

With catlike quickness, Rubin drew his Colt Cobra .38 and stepped powerfully forward, firing a round at point-blank range into the slender young man's abdomen. A scuffle ensued, and Rubin was wrestled to the cement floor. All of this was captured live on national TV. Ohlman fell to the ground in pain. Seconds later he went unconscious after an ignorant or malicious individual jumped on top of him and began pumping his abdomen supposedly to perform CPR. It was the worst course of action to take on a victim of a gunshot wound to the abdomen. It increased internal bleeding, causing Ohlman to die quickly. Like President Kelly, Ohlman was transported to the Parkland Hospital where he too was ultimately declared dead.

Meanwhile, Rubin was handcuffed and brought to a jail cell. Immediately after the incident, Woody Sorrens, the Secret Service's Special Agent in Charge of Dallas went to Rubin's cell to talk. He and a police sergeant spoke with Rubin. Jake told them that he "did it so that Jamie Kelly wouldn't have to come back to Dallas for a trial." It was a curious comment.

Chapter 52

The Cover-up Continues

"Ron told me he gave you his clothes." Lionel was confirming what he already knew.

"Yes, I have them Mr. President," answered Texas Representative Harry Gomez.

"Bring them with you when you come to Washington and drop them off with Milly. Understand?" President Jones directed.

"Yes sir," Gomez had limited information, but he knew enough about Texas politics to understand that there were times when it was wise to follow orders and not ask questions.

Lionel was one of the few in the loop regarding the importance of the Governor's clothes. Milly would have them laundered. The red substance had ·to go. The handling of the Governor's clothes would never be questioned. Why should they? After all, people in the plaza and at the hospital saw the "blood" on good old boy Conway's back. They knew he'd been hit and would swallow the cock and bull story hook, line, and sinker. Nevertheless it was an important piece of evidence that required fine tuning, just in case. Most of the key evidence was immediately seized and under the control of Harvey Hampton's FBI or the Secret Service. Hampton was doing his part. Lionel would keep his word and make special provisions to retain him as FBI director.

Assassination Point Blank

President Kelly's body was of paramount importance and it was already manipulated. Because of the point blank gunshot wound, photos and evidence of the President's skull were faked and altered in order to fit "the official story," or at least prove inconclusive. The same was true of the Governor's "injuries" and X-rays. Doctors cut a hole in the President's neck giving the appearance of a ballistic induced throat wound as a way to explain his initial choking in the car. If ever questioned, people would be reminded that a tracheotomy was required in the vicinity. Thus the wound was altered, making it too inconclusive as to what actually occurred.

Additionally Lionel was informed that a number of photos and films were taken in the plaza. Only one, a near perfect film taken by a man named Zimmersky, captured the entire event from beginning to end. Zimmersky was "lucky" enough to be positioned precisely perpendicular to the exact location of the fatal head shot. He sold his film for $100,000. Copies were made before the sale and were now in the hands of the Secret Service. The purchaser was an East Coast establishment controlled magazine owned by a Skull and Bones member, Hayden Lucy. The magazine would only publish carefully selected still frames of the event, so there was no worry about a widespread study of the film. Nevertheless, alterations were made to key frames in order to obfuscate what had transpired in the limousine. If ever questioned about the film's integrity, they would say it was damaged during handling. To protect the guilty, the participants understood the importance of keeping people's focus outside the car. As was planned in advance all evidence was to point at Ohlman. And now that Jake Rubin removed Ohlman there would be little direct testimony to refute such claims.

Chapter 53

Two Funerals

As millions lined the streets of Washington DC to mourn President Kelly's death, Lew Ohlman was buried in front of a tiny gathering on a dark, gloomy Texas day. The patsy's body was tossed into a desolate grave marked by a small headstone. Ironically, those doing the honors were news reporters turned pallbearers because there were too few family members on hand to carry the casket. Thus, the media effectively buried him twice: first, with their rushed, judgmental, and erroneous reporting, and then literally in a Fort Worth grave.

To the degree Jamie Kelly was attracting fame, sympathy, and admiration from the masses, Ohlman received the opposite - loathing, disdain, and infamy. The curious law of inverse symmetry demanded that the killer be admired as much as the patsy was detested. Deceit had won the day. The coup was successful. Texas School Book Depository or grassy knoll, the whole world was deceived. The killer was to become more famous and admired than the greatest Hollywood stars. Now, to add the icing on the cake, with her boyfriend Arion Ostratos, she would be in a position to become insanely rich as well. Turning the world upside down, the herd would admire a killer and detest an

Assassination Point Blank

innocent man. Hence, darkness was hidden in light.

***

Jamie Kelly requested that the President's body lie in repose in the East Room of the White House for twenty-four hours prior to being brought to the Capitol rotunda to lie in state for public viewing the following day. Sorrow filled the globe. Scott Kelly was despondent. He was also angry. Arion Ostratos had flown in for the funeral. Scott couldn't do much about it. Ostratos was invited by Jamie Kelly. On Ostratos's arm, Jamie walked down the Center Hall in the direction of the elevator leading to the State Floor where Scott Kelly was waiting. The sight made him sick.

A few moments later, Cliff Hillman was summoned over to the East Room, where at the doorway Jamie and Scott Kelly were getting ready to go in to view the President's body.

Hillman approached the first lady and Attorney General. "Mrs. Kelly, I received your page. What I can do?"

She was wearing a black suit and skirt with a veil over her face. Scott also wore black.

"We'd like to see the President." The room was being guarded by a group of servicemen known as the honor guard.

"Let me check with the General." Hillman replied and left to find the commander of the honor guard. He returned shortly and led them into the East Room. Ostratos waited in the Cross Hall.

The two approached the casket; Jamie kneeled solemnly while Scott stood, staring at his brother.

Jamie turned to Hillman, and asked, "Cliff, could you please bring me a pair of scissors?"

Hillman nodded, hurrying out of the room to oblige Jamie's request. Returning a short time later, he handed her the scissors. He looked away but could hear the snipping sound as she cut a lock of hair.

***

The sad day of the funeral arrived. Still in shock, the world wallowed in sorrow.

"Salute daddy," Jamie told James Jr. as the caisson passed. As instructed, young James Kelly Jr. obediently stepped forward and saluted his father's coffin. Today was his third birthday.

Scott Kelly walked with Jamie behind his brother's caisson. Military drums thumped his ears. It was what Jamie wanted. She insisted on walking. Without his older brother, Scott didn't know what his future would hold. Jamie and her children would be moving out of the White House, initially to Avery Harrison's Georgetown home.

As expected, every observer was sympathetic to Jamie Kelly, now the holy widow. Hardly spontaneous, a small inner circle had in fact planned the elaborate funeral well before the assassination. Bagpipe players, the black riderless horse following the caisson and a natural gas burning flame on top of the grave were premeditated. They even adopted a legendary name, Camelot, to refer to her husband's administration. The fairy tale name ostensibly romanticized the President's thousand days in office. However, hidden behind the romance, the occult symbolism of the fictional story was overwhelming for those who understand it, who have studied it, who can recognize it.

A central figure in the story, Queen Guinevere betrays her husband, King Arthur by having an adulterous affair with his most trusted knight Lancelot. The act leads to the downfall of the kingdom. Like Guinevere, Jamie betrayed her husband.

The ideas and planning for all the funeral arrangements, the public would be told, were amazingly put together in brilliant spontaneous and impromptu fashion by the First Lady. To further garner admiration from the public, during the funeral procession she insisted on walking in full view behind the casket instead of riding in a car. It worked like a charm. The world was fascinated by her act of extraordinary courage. The First Lady would now be thought of sympathetically as a hero as well. To the public, she was now the holy widow. In reality, she was the Black Widow. Adding to the madness, the funeral was being held on exactly the third birthday of young James Kelly Jr.

With the shock over the death of the president, few stopped to ponder why Jamie had no concern about snipers in Washington D.C. on the day of the funeral. It was the same reason she had known it was unnecessary for her to duck as the limousine made its death ride through Dealey Plaza. Such questions would not be asked, certainly not by the mainstream media. Instead, on this day the first lady's courage and the wonderful solidarity of the participants, including international heads of states and dignitaries, would be emphasized. None would ever conceive the possibility that a point-blank assassin and accomplices would actually now be participating in the procession. The traitors walked confidently, without fear of prosecution or a rifle toting assassin.

In the cemetery, leading up to the grave, nine bagpipe players marched slowly and played an eerie tune.

Nine hides 666 in the occult (9=8+1 & 18=6+6+6).

It is the number of finality, and a reversed six which is said to be the number of the perfected man, the illuminated man. At the gravesite a Presidential memorial with an eternal flame was constructed. In the center point of the stone circle was a flame, the hermaphroditic signature symbol of the Brotherhood. President Kelly's grave for them was a trophy signifying victory over their enemy and capped by their magical symbol representing illuminated man and the light of Lucifer. A New World Order was indeed coming into view.

Chapter 54

The Gravesite

The Catholic Church was known at times to save a part of a body such as a bone, lock of hair, or even a finger nail. However such practices were typically reserved for saints. The body part would then be placed in the church named after the saint being honored. Unbeknownst to Scott Kelly, the lock of hair clipped from his brother's head was intended for use in a curse against him. Arion Ostratos requested his lover obtain a hair sample from the President.

At President Kelly's gravesite, while others were not paying attention, Arion Ostratos nonchalantly reached to the ground and gathered a small amount of dirt. He scooped it into a tiny vial, similar to a perfume sample vial, hidden in his hand. Then, using a second empty identical vial, he opened the cap and shook it slightly so that it became filled with the air located near Kelly's grave. With air from the new location now inside, he replaced the cap. All of this was done in a matter of seconds and went undetected. Earlier, Jamie had discreetly handed him a small lock of her dead husband's hair which he requested. The hair was already hidden in a third vial inside his suit jacket. Now he possessed the essential ingredients he was instructed to obtain.

Through contacts made via his close
friendship with the President of Haiti, Arion
had arranged for a future gathering of voodoo
high priests. Together, they would conduct an
occult ritual curse designed to eliminate the
last of their enemies, starting with the young
Attorney General. After the younger brother's
demise Arion and his lover could marry.

Epilogue

"Ah, shit!" President Jones yelled, after he took an awkward swing with his #1 wood off the white tees. The golf ball sliced and bounced from the right edge of the right side of the fairway into the higher grass of the rough.

"That's not a bad spot, Lionel. You still have a shot from there," assured Governor Conway as he took a few practice swings. The men had their bags clipped to an electric golf cart parked nearby. Lionel had instructed his Secret Service men to stay far enough away so he and Conway could converse in private.

It was a humid July day during the summer of 1967 and nearly four years had passed since Kelly's death. Exactly one week after the assassination, Jones had created a Commission, headed by Chief Justice of the Supreme Court, Earnest Warner, to "investigate" the murder. Ten months later, the Commission, which consisted almost entirely of members of the Secret Brotherhood, concluded in an 888 page report, that President Kelly was killed by Lew Hardy Ohlman. Ohlman was portrayed as a deranged left-wing malcontent who acted alone. Pointing to Ohlman was the Commission's sole purpose from the beginning. The Commission went out of its way to ignore or discount any evidence that did not point to Lew Hardy Ohlman.

During their investigation, the Commission received a call from a Benjamin Brown, the Secret Service agent who had warned about dangers to President Kelly before the assassination. He stated that he had more information that might be helpful to the Commission. It wasn't long before news of Brown's call reached the architects of the conspiracy. They couldn't have an agent exposing the Secret Service and causing the public to even consider the possibility of incompetence, or worse yet, an inside job. At the time of his call, Brown didn't realize the Commission wasn't searching for the truth but was instead created to protect the guilty.

To keep the truth buried, the conspirators needed to jettison Brown, so they decided to set him up. They figured if they could frame him for a crime, and send him to prison, nobody would want to talk with, much less believe, a jailed felon. That is, even if he was still willing and able to tell what he knew, he would be discredited. Lionel was happy when Brown was out of the way.

Conway teed off and hit a shot not much better than Lionel's. The ball came to a rest in the same general area of the rough, about 10 yards further.

The two lanky Texans climbed into the cart. Lionel steered it to travel in the shade, under a line of trees on the right side of the fairway. He slowly drove toward the two white golf balls.

"So what is the latest status of that former Negro agent?" Conway asked. Conway knew Brown refused a job with the IRS just five days prior to the assassination. The position would have changed his identity and would have made it nearly impossible for him to come forward as a reliable witness. After the assassination, when Brown started making phone calls the conspirators knew they had a problem and setup their frame job. Conway lost track of the man.

"You mean that fellow Brown? He's still in jail, in a psychiatric ward in Springfield, Missouri," Lionel smiled, forgetting momentarily about his lousy shot. "He won't be out for years."

"That's what he gets for opening his big mouth. He needed to be put in his place," replied Conway. "I understand you promoted Hillman to Special Agent in Charge (SAIC) of your protection," Conway grinned, thinking back to Hillman's role on 11-22-63.

"Yes, I did." Lionel laughed, thinking about how Hillman was being hailed a hero in the media for his valiant attempt to save the lives of President Kelly and the First Lady. Hillman was even given a citation in the US Treasury Building for his bravery less than two weeks after the assassination. Meanwhile, the honest Brown was now a convicted felon rotting in jail. Brown, totally sane, was being evaluated in a psych ward while the two psychopaths were out playing golf. Proud of their work, the two psychopaths laughed and continued their game.

***

Immediately following President Kelly's death, Jamie and her children moved out of the White House into Avery Harrison's Georgetown home on N street. About a month later Jamie bought a house across the street from Harrison's. Madeline Murphy stayed on as Jamie's secretary. Madeline learned that the new house had an eerie past. It had been the setting of a mystery novel, *The Simple Way of Poison,* by Zenith Brown, whose pen name was Leslie Ford. What was the mystery's plot? Spousal murder and betrayal! In it, the wife murders her husband, greed being a motive.

During her time working for Jamie in the new house, Madeline noticed that for some reason Jamie hadn't displayed any pictures of James Kelly. She and her children didn't live in the house long. By September of 1964 she decided to move to New York. Madeline was no longer needed and received her notice of termination from Jamie by telephone. After that time, Madeline kept up with her through the newspapers.

There were circumstances surrounding the assassination that still bothered Madeline. After the assassination, Jamie had asked her to type up a letter to the Secretary of the Treasury stating that President Kelly had intended to leave the highest possible recommendations in the files of the Secret Service agents before he left office, and that he wanted each of the agents to be given the chance for a promotion. The request made no sense. Madeline wondered if the president ever said such a thing. At the time of his death he was already campaigning for a second term in office. If he won, which he planned to do, he would be around five more years. Consequently, why would he be thinking of the promotion of Secret Service agents 5 years before he left office? Madeline sensed something out of line.

She thought about some of the other members of the Kelly staff. Most had since quit. She knew the reason. Now without President Kelly, it was even worse. Melancholy ruled the day. After his death, it wasn't long before the help started to have difficulties with Jamie. She was cheap, and she never cared about others until they were quitting. Employee morale deteriorated.

Mae Smith had gone back to England. Before she left, she asked Jamie if she could have something to remember President Kelly. Jamie gave her a shirt.

For some time after the assassination, Ellen Lakeland was busy working to create and organize the Archives and the new James Kelly library. Jamie didn't seem too concerned with preserving her husband's legacy, at least not when it came to the library. She even asked Ellen what was taking so long in archiving and setting up the library. "I could put it all on index cards in one afternoon," Jamie told her, sarcastically.

Ellen told Madeline that right after Kelly's death, Lionel Jones callously ordered Ellen to get all of James Kelly's "junk" out of the White House. In contrast, he had a much different tone with Jamie, telling her she could take as much time as necessary.

Naturally, the whole world wondered what the future would hold for President Kelly's brother. Would he run for president?

***

Thirty years later on a gray, cloudy, and unusually cold afternoon in Washington D.C., Grant Vadala roamed through Rock Creek Cemetery. He was on his way to a small familiar headstone to pay his respect at the grave of a boyhood friend who died in World War II, five decades earlier. He always tried to visit his friend's grave at least once a year. He wore layers of clothing which the chilly breeze could not penetrate. He walked slowly to his destination.

Now in his late sixties, Grant was spending more time contemplating his life and the people he had encountered along the way. Passing the gravestones he began to reflect back, especially about his step sister, Jamie, who had met her demise just the day before. Grant didn't feel bad. Jamie was a true lover of none and a worshipper of money, which she loved more than fame. The media had built her up and made her more famous and adored than any lead actress in Hollywood. Her pictures were on the covers of nearly every major magazine. She was a master of deception and an elite actress on a different stage. Despite the public's spellbound awe, Grant recognized her as the worst kind of actress - a monumental counterfeit.

He remembered how after the death of the President his step sister's behavior became more overtly outrageous and yet somehow accepted. At one point, it was so reckless that she was simultaneously discussing marriage with Arion Ostratos, allegedly having an affair with her brother-in-law, the married Scott Kelly, and meeting the former Deputy Secretary of Defense, Ross Gilliam for a tryst on the beaches of the Yucatan peninsula. This last indiscretion resulted in some embarrassing photographs. Gilliam happened to be yet another shadowy figure from Yale. Grant pondered the connections. Certain ubiquitous Yale alumni seemed to turn up in strange places.

He remembered her bizarre, controlling behavior in her attempt to monopolize the written rendition of the president's death by hiring a well-known author and then threatening to sue a second author who also wanted to write a similar book on the assassination. Strangely, she ended up filing a law suit against the first author, asking the court to issue an injunction to prevent the book's publication unless changes were made. She claimed the material was solely intended for her husband's presidential library.

At the very end, it was well known, even to the public, that Jamie was sick with cancer. Grant had received word from family members that the cancer had spread to her brain. He was told that she had a hole drilled in her skull so that Radium or some other element could be inserted. He didn't realize that instead of something being inserted in Jamie's skull, something had been removed: the electronic implants used in MK-ULTRA mind control experiments and special projects.

He thought of the assassination and how it always seemed suspicious to him and that the investigation left more questions than answers. It was conveniently odd that Jamie seemed to benefit most from the death of the President. As he gazed around Rock Creek Cemetery it brought to mind the nearby Rock Creek Park and the ex-wife of a CIA official, Annie Myers, who was mysteriously murdered less than a year after the Kelly assassination. Bob Angler was found in the dead woman's apartment looking for her diary. Grant wondered how her death related to that of the President.

Finally, arriving at his destination, he sat on a nearby bench and thought of his boyhood friend who died in Iwo Jima. He wondered if World War II had been avoidable, like the disastrous war in Vietnam that Jones started. If so, he wondered whether his friend's death had also been avoidable. After ten minutes or so, he stood and slowly wandered past a nearby headstone. He stopped to read its inscription.

It read:

> *What is truth?*
> *Truth is the only constant.*
> *Without it there is no happiness, there is*
> *no respect.*
> *Truth cannot be bottled up forever.*
> *No, it will eventually rise to the surface.*
> *For what is concealed today will be*
> *revealed one day.*

President Kelly had been dead over 30 years. Vadala wondered if the full truth surrounding the man's death would ever be known. Then he recalled a quote from another President, who also fell by assassination, James A. Garfield: *The truth will set you free, but first it will make you miserable.* That's probably what will happen when the truth finally does come out, he thought, as he turned to leave the cemetery.

Made in the USA
Middletown, DE
20 December 2014